The Bone Heart

IVY WARREN

The Bone Heart

Written by Ivy Warren
Edited by EB Editorial Services
Cover Art by Polina Stoycheva

*Content Warning: death, violence, explicit sex scenes,
attempted sexual assault*

Ivy Warren

This book is for every reader who falls for the villain, but wishes they were gay.

The Bone Heart

Chapter One

At least the last time I spent this long on my knees on a cold floor, I had my lover's thighs to warm my ears. My lips tugged into a smile despite the chill. I pulled my cap down low and hugged my thin coat tighter around myself. My disguise was loose enough that it hid the curves that would give me away, and it felt like the cold air was seeping into every gap. Even though it had been almost a whole day, the boy clothes I wore still felt wrong on my skin. Coarse fabric brushed against the insides of my thighs in a way it never had before.

I shifted uncomfortably and had to remind myself that it was hardly forever. A few days of deceit and danger and then I would be free. We would be free. The thought of escaping my gilded cage of a life was the only thing keeping me from abandoning this miserable adventure already. Thunder rolled out across the sea and, even here, in the warehouse where I had stashed myself amongst the crates, the tremors shook my bones. Mother had always warned me to stay away from the port where the unsavory types lurked. But then again, in her opinion a great deal of things were unsavory, I thought with a trace of old bitterness rising up inside me. That was why I was doing this, after all. My lover and I would never be accepted. Could never be accepted. Our only hope to be together was to flee far away from here and never look back.

"Be brave, my pearl," my lover had said this morning, kissing my forehead before furrowing her own brow at my disguise. It had been her idea and she had picked it out for me, but it seemed the scruffy garments chafed at her as much as they were chafing me. Madame Chevalier preferred me in silk.

I smiled at her term of endearment. My pearl. Even from the first time we met, she had never called me Elise.

It had been daylight when I had wormed my way through the open window of the dockside warehouse and the sun should still have been visible above the horizon, but the black clouds that had swept in darkened the sky like midnight. I told myself that the darkness would help hide me and that it was a good thing, but the voice in the back of my mind whispered of ill omens. No matter my nerves, the shuffling of activity at the warehouse doors was my signal to move. I could not delay a moment longer. I had put off this part until the very last second as the mere thought of it had my heart pounding and my palms perspiring.

The travel chest's hinges made no sound when I eased the lid open. They had been well oiled by Madame's ever-present manservant, Gerald. He never spoke to me directly, but the slight smirk on the older man's face whenever he opened the door for me or brought me tea left little doubt that he knew that we were not simply painting during all those hours spent in Madame Chevalier's studio. When I voiced my doubts, however, Madame assured me of his discretion. He had been with her for years and she never had reason to doubt his loyalty. I had not asked if he would be accompanying us to the Thoredian Isles, the idyllic patch of paradise where we could make our life together. I hoped not. I wanted her all to myself.

I did have to give Gerald credit for the chest, though. He had ensured it would be comfortable for me as I hid. The inside was cushioned while strategically drilled holes allowed me to breathe fresh air. A small package of food and water was tucked in the corner for my journey. Everything was ready. I closed my eyes to the sound of voices echoing as sailors called instructions to each other.

They were getting closer. Instinctively, I tried to gather my skirts, but my questing fingers met only the rough texture of my pants. It was now or never. I took one last deep breath and stepped into the chest. Once I closed the lid, that was it. I would be loaded onto The Lydia, a merchant ship set for Mulla, the largest of the Thoredian Isles. Mulla, where my lover would join me. Where we could finally be together. I let hope overtake my apprehension. This was what I wanted. What I needed. Her. Us. The lid closed with a soft clunk and I latched it from the inside with trembling fingers.

Although I had tried out the chest when it was first presented to me, curled up on my side and giggling in Madame's bedchambers, I never imagined the temperature it would reach inside. I had only a small bottle of water, and I was truly afraid I would run out far sooner than I expected. The sailors and merchant's men worked quickly, and I could hear the scraping and grunting as the crates next to me were lifted and carried away to be loaded onto the ship. Every time the sounds grew closer, my stomach twisted with a thrill of fear. Stowing away was, after all, a crime.

When I had confided my fears in Madame Chevalier, she reminded me that every time we lay together, we broke the law. That the risk of someone finding out was why we were running away. That and my impending marriage, of course. At the time, it had made sense but now, with the scuffling of boots mere inches from my head, I was filled with regrets. I had to bite my fist to keep from crying out as the handles were grasped and the chest, with me tucked inside it, was lifted into the air.

Over the next hour, encased in my cushioned chest, I was picked up, dropped, slid across the floor and, at one point, I was certain that someone was sitting on the lid until, at last, the footsteps faded into silence.

I let out a shuddering breath. There was no going back now. There had never been any going back. Not since the day I met Madame Chevalier.

The Day We Met

"Elise, darling?" Mother called. "We have a guest."

I smoothed my skirts. She was here.

Madame Ismay Chevalier. Tall, intimidating and utterly wonderous. I had seen her work at the new gallery opening in town, and it had taken my breath away almost as much as the woman had herself. She stood with such poise and elegance. Her hair was impeccably pinned and, although it was now streaked by gray, it must have once been richly dark like mine. I wanted her to look at me. To speak to me. I wanted to be her.

I was introduced to her as a budding painter myself, I could only stutter vague pleasantries. How she must have thought me a fool. None were so shocked as I when she asked to view my work. Of course, I had accepted in an instant, blabbering like a child.

Now that she was here, in my home, I regretted having spoken a single word. What was she going to think of my inexperienced paintings? She would say something placating as to not be impolite, and then she would leave and never come back and wonder why she ever wasted the time. It took all my willpower to make my feet move in the direction of Mother's voice. My own personal humiliation was nothing compared to if I embarrassed my mother with a lack of manners.

When I entered the summer room with its wicker armchairs and decorative orange trees, my head was light with apprehension. I thought I truly might faint for a moment. Mother stood at the far window, gesturing out across the manicured lawn and most likely discussing her plans for a new water feature. Water features were all the rage this season.

And then there was her. Madame Chevalier was nodding along and turned when she saw me enter. I was sure I imagined that her eyes lit up. Surely, she could not be that pleased to see me?

"Ah, here she is." She smiled widely, the corners of her eyes crinkling, and offered me her hand. An emerald sparkled from her finger.

"Madame," I murmured, bobbing a curtsey. "May I offer you some refreshments?"

"I thought I might first see your work."

I startled. I thought I would have more time to collect my thoughts but, with the way she and Mother were looking at me expectantly, it was clear I was not to have that time. My mouth dried up and I had to cough before I could speak.

"Indeed," I said, trying to hide my nerves. "I have prepared some pieces in the morning room."

"I will have tea waiting for when you are finished," Mother said.

She left us alone then and I felt the full force of Madame's attention on me. I quickly led her to where I had set up my favorite pieces so that she could look at something other than myself.

Her heels clicked on the hard floor as she approached each one, pausing at length, tapping a long finger on her chin. My insides felt like they had been carved up and put on show. I twisted my hands in the fabric of my skirts. I desperately wanted to know what she thought and, at the same time, wanted to throw the drop cloths over each and every canvas to shield them from her.

"You have a good eye," she murmured.

"Oh, my goodness, thank you—" I gushed but she silenced me with a wave.

"But you lack discipline. See here?" She gestured to a still life of a flower bouquet—one that a young man had brought me— and tutted. I stared at the smears on the canvas in dismay. How could I have not seen the inelegant rush of the brushstrokes? How could I have presented this to her? My cheeks were aflame.

If Madame noticed my shame, she was kind enough not to address it.

"I have been contemplating taking on a student. Someone with talent."

My mortification forgotten, I held my breath. That would be a dream come true. A proper teacher. Someone to show me how to truly see things. How to create beautiful things. Someone who saw that I had something to offer the world.

"Would you accept?"

"I would!" I blurted.

She smiled at my eagerness and took a step closer.

"My fees can be…steep."

"My father would pay them," I assured her. Father had always been supportive of my artistic pursuits, and my mother was desperate for me to integrate more with Beauris' high society. As the daughter of the Duke of Beauris, I was granted invitations as a matter of principle but Mother was quick to remind me how simply rubbing elbows with the correct people could get one ahead in life.

"Ah, this here…" Madame Chevalier gestured to my self-portrait. "Now this is just exquisite."

"It is nothing," I stammered.

"Shh," she said, closing the distance between us so that I had to tilt my head to look up at her. "Never undermine your talents."

Up close, I caught the scent of her perfume. Jasmine with a touch of sweet vanilla. It was rich and sensual and fit her perfectly.

"I think together we could make exquisite things." Her steel gray eyes met mine and one fingertip lifted my chin making my pulse race. "Don't you think?"

Chapter Two

I clearly had overestimated my ability to stay curled up in a chest for hours on end. With Madame's encouraging words, I truly thought I could do it but, in the end, I simply could not stay still.

I did not have a timepiece or a light to read one if I had, but I would have estimated it had been less than two hours before I snuck out of the chest. Madame had always said from the very beginning that I lacked patience and discipline, and I was proving her right once again. However, I reasoned that if I stayed in the cargo area, then no one would find me. I also realized that I could not have stayed in the chest the entire time without needing to relieve myself at some point, although that thought had not occurred to me whilst planning this adventure.

I was cautious as I lifted the lid and clambered out, pausing every few seconds to listen. The cargo area was as I expected—dark, cramped and full of crates and barrels. I could have still been in the dockside warehouse for all I knew, except the curve of the wooden walls and the rocking motion told me otherwise. I was aboard a ship. I sent a silent prayer of thanks that nothing heavy had been stacked on top of my chest, trapping me inside. I shuddered as I found myself a space between crates to settle in once I had stretched out my legs. Excitement sparked in my belly. I was at sea. I had truly done it. This was the start of the rest of my life.

I let pleasant thoughts of island paradise distract me for a while, but I should have known myself better. It had been the lament of many a governess that I could never simply be content and to sit quietly. During my schooling, I had decorated my books with drawings in the margins to pass the time but now I did not even have my sketchbook with me. All my treasured possessions had been secretly packed and sent ahead, but everything else had to be left behind so that no one suspected my escape. I would miss them terribly, but Madame had quelled all my worries. We would buy new things, make new memories, carve out a new life for ourselves. I let myself smile. We would have all the time in the world instead of a few stolen hours disguised as painting lessons.

Soon, I found myself wandering around the cargo hold, trying to pry open some of the boxes to see what was inside. None of them yielded to my efforts.

I was about to start looking for some kind of tool that would let me open them and investigate properly when the sound of footsteps startled me. I thought no one would come down here and panic instantly rose in my chest. I darted one way and then another but there was nowhere to run to. I was trapped. Ducking down behind one of the crates just as a pair of boots thudded down the stairs saved me from being spotted immediately and I crawled on my hands and knees into the shadows, my heart hammering.

An incomprehensible shout came from above and the man simply laughed and called back, "Aye!"

He was coming closer. I huddled into the smallest ball I possibly could and peeked out as he passed my hiding place. He was as tanned and as burly as one would expect of a sailor. The buttons of his vest strained as he moved and each of his arms were as thick as my entire torso and ridged with scars. I could not see his face as he was faced away from me but if he turned...All that was between us was one crate. One crate that barely hid me. If he turned, he would see me. He *was* going to see me. I was going to be discovered. Oh lord, what would they do to me? Would I be arrested? Mother would die of the shame.

I had to get back to my travelling chest. I had been a fool to leave it and even more a fool for wandering so far. If I could get back, I would be safe.

I was just about to make my move when a floorboard behind me creaked. My heart flew into my mouth. I tried to spin around but, before I could move, a pair of heavy hands landed on my shoulders.

"What've we got here?"

I shrieked and tried to scramble away, but the hands yanked me backwards like I weighed nothing at all. My feet flew out from under me and I landed on my back, the air knocked from my lungs. Gasping, I stared up with watering eyes at not one but two leering faces.

"A stowaway, is it?" The second man was barefoot, explaining why I had not heard his approach. His long, ropey hair was bound up in a red bandana, and a gold medallion glittered at his throat. He appeared more curious than angry at least –not like the other sailor. I flinched as his thick eyebrows pulled together in a scowl.

My gaze darted from one to the other, adrenaline pounding in my veins. Any plea for mercy I could have made got lost somewhere in my throat as the angry one reached down to grab me. I kicked out at him reflexively, but he knocked my feet away and flipped me onto my belly. I scrambled on my hands and knees, trying to get away, but a boot planted firmly between my shoulder blades pinned me to the floor as effectively as a butterfly to a board. I had never in my life been manhandled in such a manner.

"Release me!" My voice came out as a terrified squeak.

Dazed and scared beyond belief, I only caught snippets of their conversation about what to do with me as I scraped my nails against the floor in an attempt to pull myself out from under his boot.

"You heard the captain as well as I did," growled the one pinning me.

The weight suddenly left my back.

Blinded by the tears in my eyes and still frozen by the shock of being caught, I did not realize I had stopped trying to get away until rough hands under my arms and around my ankles had lifted me clear off the floor. To them, I seemed to weigh nothing at all and they made quick work of carrying me up onto the deck.

As I was lugged out of the hold, the salt spray of the sea settled on my cheeks and eyelashes. At one time, I may have found it refreshing had the change of scenery not been accompanied by the terrifying realization that I was being carried to the railing.

At the thought of being thrown to a watery grave, my voice fought itself free.

"No! Please! Release me!" I gasped, wiggling frantically, but received only laughter in response until one of my captors, the angry one, slipped on the wet planks and lost his grip on my legs.

I kicked at him once more, still trying to escape the other's grasp. My arms slid from my coat, and I almost managed to get free as I shucked it off. The ropey-haired man swore but managed to catch a hold of me again.

"What's this then?" A thoroughly annoyed voice sailed over to us.

I hardly dared to breathe as the men paused in trying to wrestle me to the side of the ship and snapped to attention.

"Found a stowaway, Captain Halliwell."

Oh, thank goodness, I thought as I sagged in relief. The captain would put a stop to this madness.

As Captain Halliwell stalked towards us, I gasped. The captain's features were obscured in silhouette as she loomed over me, but it was undeniable. The captain was a woman. I had never even heard of a female sailor, let alone a female captain.

She reached out to yank the cap from my head, grasp a fistful of my long, dark hair that I had hidden under it, and jerk my face up so that she could look at me properly. I winced as pain shot through my scalp.

"A girl?" The woman made a tired, disgruntled noise. "We don't have time for this."

"Please! Wait! I must be on the wrong ship!" I gasped.

Lying was not my strong suit but perhaps if I could make her believe that I was simply mistaken, then I would not be handed to the authorities. I had to try. I could not be arrested, I simply could not.

"Yes, yes you are." Captain Halliwell leered. "Boys, help her leave, will you?"

My stomach flipped. The thought of being arrested was bad enough, I could hardly process that the captain really meant to do away with me instead. I thrashed in the sailors' grip as she made to turn away, seemingly done with the unwanted distraction my presence had caused.

"I made a mistake! Please, will you not help me?"

"A girl dressed as a boy did not mean to stow away? Do you take me for a fool?" Captain Halliwell hissed. "Get this wretch off my ship now."

I was reaching desperation. If I could not lie my way out or appeal to the captain's mercy, then perhaps I could appeal to her coin purse.

"Wait!" I shrieked. "My father is a duke! He will reward you if you take me home!"

It was the only card I had left to play. If she took me up on it, I would return home in disgrace and never be allowed to leave the house again, but that was far preferable to being tossed off the side of a ship. My parents would never know what happened to me if I died here.

"Which duke?"

I had caught her interest. My hope was like a bubble in my chest that swelled with every breath.

"Duke Barnett of Beauris! Please! I am so sorry! Please do not throw me over!" My throat was threatening to close up over my desperate begging and I willed it to hold out.

"I know of the duke." Captain Halliwell tilted her head, scanning my face with dark, keen eyes. A shark's eyes. "I doubt you are lying about your father. You have his look about you. Will he pay for you though?"

"He will—!"

"Quiet!"

I clamped my mouth shut as the captain's eyes raked over me once again and she stroked her chin as if deep in thought.

"Bring her to my cabin. I've got a few questions for our little stowaway."

Captain Halliwell turned on her heel and I was dragged after her, stumbling over my own feet and momentarily light-headed with relief. I had a chance.

I was hauled into the captain's cabin and dumped in a chair opposite an imposing desk. The two sailors who had caught me left, each giving the captain a respectful nod. I had never seen men defer to a woman like this and I had no idea what to make of it. Whoever this strange woman was, as captain she held my life in her hands.

I rubbed at my arms where I would surely have bruises from the sailor's tight grip before I instinctively adjusted myself to sit up straight and cross my ankles. Captain Halliwell perched on the end of her desk in front of me, staring. It felt like she was trying to see through my skin to my very bones. My skin prickled and meeting her eye proved an impossible task. As composed as my posture may have been, my heart rattled around my ribs like a caged animal. One wrong word—one wrong look—and I would still find myself in an unmarked watery grave. Just because the captain had stopped her brutes from tossing me overboard for now, did not mean she would not change her mind.

"What is your name?"

Words stuck in my throat, and I found myself having to swallow before answering.

"Elise," I managed hoarsely. "Elise Barnett."

"Who else is on my ship?"

"No one. I am alone."

The captain slid from the desk with cat-like agility and drew to her full height before me. Soft, leather-gloved fingertips captured my chin and tilted my face up.

"Elise Barnett," she purred, cocking her head and staring into my eyes. "What the hell are you doing on my ship?"

I bit my lip.

Again, words failed me. Her eyes were such a deep brown that they were almost black. Her tanned skin told of many months at sea as did the sun-bleached strands in her brown hair. She was definitely older than I, but not as old as my mother. Perhaps in her thirties? Her coat was high quality velvet and, with its gold embroidery, would not have been out of place at the finest establishments of Beauris had it not been for the fact that it was entirely untailored for her shape. Her jewelry too, glittering from her ears and at her throat, was tasteful and finely made. She did not fit the crude image of a sailor that I had in my mind. In fact, I would have found her startlingly attractive if she had not been looking at me like she wanted to devour me whole.

"I asked you a question." Her fingers tightened on my chin.

Doubt wormed at my mind. A female captain would have been the talk of the town in Beauris, but not a word of this Captain Halliwell had reached me. The Lydia was supposed to be a reputable merchant vessel that was known to the port. There was no way her captain would be a woman and no one would have gossiped about it.

"I believe I am aboard the wrong ship," I blurted, trying to hide my wince. "I was supposed to board a merchant ship called The Lydia, but…" I trailed off as the captain threw back her head and laughed. "Did I say something amusing?" I asked, unnerved by the sudden change in her mood.

"Not in the slightest," she snapped, back to her sneer. "The Lydia, you say?"

Madame Chevalier had planned it all out so carefully. I must have made a mistake somewhere. Or had the sailors loaded my chest onto the wrong vessel? She had talked me through all the details. Patiently listing it all while combing my hair as I sat at her feet, fretting. I had to travel secretly. I was too recognizable, plus my father would send people looking when my bedroom was found empty in the morning. She had sent some of my belongings already ahead—my paintings, some clothes and most of my jewelry—and she would meet me one day after I landed in Mulla. She had made it sound so simple.

Would she know I was on the wrong ship already? Or would she only know something was wrong when I did not appear to meet her? She would hire an army to find me, I was sure of it, but would it already be too late?

"This *is* The Lydia." The captain held arms out as if she were presenting it to me. "Well, sometimes she is anyway, when we wish to be discrete. Her true name is the Bone Heart."

Chapter Three

"Bone...Heart?" I echoed. The name stirred something in the back of my memory, but a more pressing issue sprang forth, one that made my mouth dry up as if I had taken sand into it. If the Lydia was a false name, then perhaps its destination had also been fabricated.

"Is this ship still set for the Thoredian Isles? For Mulla?" I asked as dread slid down my spine.

"Not even close." Captain Halliwell's lips curled into a cruel, mocking smile as my heart sank. "Running away, were you?"

"I...uh..." Heat flooded my face. "I was to meet someone."

The captain caressed my cheek. "A special someone?"

I jerked away from her touch.

"That is none of your concern," I snapped and then slammed my mouth shut as the captain's expression turned predatory. She gripped the arms of my chair and loomed over me, inches from my face. It was a cruel trick of an unfeeling world to give someone so dreadful such perfect, full lips. My breath hitched. Even as they curled back in a snarl, I could not stop my eyes from darting to them.

"Everything on my ship concerns me," she growled. "So tell me, little stowaway, if you were running away, why would your father pay to get you back?"

I swallowed hard. "He will pay. He...he was going to marry me to Mr. Thompson of Thompson and Sons. The son, that is. They are to be in business together. Without the strength of a marriage, the deal could fall apart."

I was babbling. Mother always scolded me for babbling when I got excited, it seemed I did so when in fear for my life too.

The proposal. That had been what started this unfortunate sequence of events. We had always talked of running away together but, when I turned up unannounced at Madame's townhouse in tears after learning I was to be married, we made our plans to escape.

"A pretty little pawn, then." Captain Halliwell leaned back against her desk, seemingly lost in thought. "Are you worth the trouble, though?"

I knew the question was rhetorical and she did not actually require a reply. I shivered, lamenting the loss of my coat. The rivers of sweat that had run down my back during my earlier struggle now chilled me to a sticky mess. I was not one for physical exertion at the best of times, and the sensation was both highly unusual and unpleasant.

"I am. I promise! I—"

"You will address me as 'Captain' or you will lose your tongue," Captain Halliwell snapped.

I blinked at her in shock. Life on a ship was notoriously dangerous, but I doubted any respectable captain would actually mutilate a passenger for simply neglecting a term of address. Then again, I was hardly a passenger, I reminded myself.

The correct response would be 'yes, Captain'," she said, the low snarl in her voice leaving no doubt as to her sincerity.

"Yes, Captain," I peeped. I already had strong doubts that this captain was the respectable kind. Regardless, both my lover and I were too fond of my tongue to even entertain the risk of losing it.

"And you do not speak unless I request it." Captain

Halliwell paced the length of her desk as she spoke. "You will follow all and any orders. You will be as meek and untroublesome as a mouse."

My heart soared and I almost sobbed in relief. I would not die today.

"Do you understand?"

"Yes, Captain."

"You will work for your place to sleep and whatever scraps I deign to throw you."

My smile faltered.

I will dictate a letter to your father, and you will sign it. If the ransom is paid to my contact, we'll let you off next time we sail anywhere near Beauris. If not, I'll feed you to the sharks."

"Ransom? Wait, no, you must take me home right away—"

Her backhanded blow knocked me out of my chair. My head smacked off the luxurious rug. Disoriented and blinking tears from my eyes, I cried out as the captain yanked me upright by my hair.

"Never forget your place," she hissed. "I am the captain, and you are less than nothing while you are aboard my ship. Do not presume to tell me what I must do."

I was unsure if I was crying from the pain or the shock. I had never been struck before except as a child being rapped across the palms with a ruler by a strict governess. My reply was lost in a whimpering sob as she pulled farther so that I was bent backwards, staring up at the ceiling, my throat exposed. "And I believe I told you to address me as Captain."

"Yes, Captain!" I gasped, tears streaming unbidden down my cheeks. I had gravely misunderstood the situation. This woman was utterly insane.

"I doubt you'll even last until I can collect my money," she scoffed. "Weak, pampered, soft. Too soft for the sea. Too sweet. Poor little sweetpea."

I gritted my teeth as she guided me back to the chair and finally released my hair. I had thought having my hair pulled into various intricate knots with pins by my lady's maid had been painful. I massaged my scalp as fresh tears rolled down my cheeks.

"I am going to ask you again. Why are you on my ship?"

"I...I was to travel to Mulla to meet...to meet my lover."

Now was not the time for lies, not when my very life depended on the whims of this madwoman.

"An inappropriate lover?" Her lips quirked in amusement.

I nodded my head miserably. The scandal would have ruined my family if I had let my relationship with Madame Chevalier become common gossip. Abandoning my engagement, however initially harmful, could be explained away. I had left a letter to my mother when I left, suggesting she could tell people I had taken ill and left for the countryside. I had also asked that no-one come looking for me. I sorely regretted my words now.

"Why are you not travelling together?" The captain narrowed her eyes. "I swear, if I find another stowaway on my ship..."

I shook my head. "I swear it, Captain, I am alone."

"How did you get on my ship?"

"I hid inside a chest."

"Which chest? Tell me exactly."

I described it in as much detail as I could. At that moment, I very much wanted to climb back inside that chest and disappear. Curl up in the dark and emerge on a beautiful, secluded island just like Madame had promised me. Where we could be together.

The captain interrupted my story of breaking into the warehouse to swear viciously. I had never heard such language from a woman, and I could not help but stare in shock.

"So, someone knows where I store my wares, enough about my business to know how to get them on the roster and the name I use for my ship in port..." Her expression was murderous. "We are on a tight schedule but, afterwards, I will make sure we pay this lover of yours a visit. This is a problem I could have done without."

"No! You cannot—" I gasped, meaning to plead mercy for Madame's involvement but the captain's fingers found my throat and squeezed.

"You forget yourself yet again," she hissed. "I have granted you your life and, for that, it is mine. This was no spur of the moment plan. Who is this lover and what do they know of me and my ship? I want names, stowaway."

"I could not give her Madame's name. I could not put her in danger. After all she had done for me, after all our talk of what our life together could be, I could not. I would be her brave pearl. I kept my lips pressed together.

For some reason, that made Captain Halliwell smile.

"You seem to be under the illusion that you have some choice in the matter, sweetpea. Maybe back in Beauris, as the daughter of the duke, you might have had choices. Maybe you would have had the luxury of protecting your precious lover. Not on my ship. I'll make this simple for you. Talk, and I'll let you keep breathing."

Her grip was suddenly iron. Not even a whisper of a breath made it to my lungs. I clawed uselessly at her wrist, panic overtaking any other instincts. My kicking legs could not seem to make contact even though she was looming right over me.

Shadows had started to creep into the corners of my vision when she finally released me. I fell from my chair to my knees, coughing and spluttering in a most undignified fashion, spit flying from my lips as I sucked air into my aching chest. I rubbed my throat, half-expecting to feel it caved in from the force of her grip.

I gave up on trying not to cry. My shoulders shook with sobs, partly in relief and partly in fear of this woman who could so callously choke me half to death. Captain Halliwell stood over me, an impassionate look decorating her face.

"You are a brute!" I gasped.

"I am a pirate, sweetpea. And I want a name."

Pirate.

The word echoed around my head. Pirate. Pirate. *Pirate*. I was not on any merchant vessel at all. I was on a pirate ship. Oh Lord.

The Bone Heart. I suddenly remembered where I had heard the name. One of my father's associates was lamenting about a lost shipment at breakfast one day, and he had rattled off a list of prominent ship names in anger as he stabbed at his sausages. The Misfortune...The Salted Lady...The Flying Storm...and The Bone Heart.

Captain Halliwell waited until my sobs had dissipated enough for me to speak, even though the words were punctuated with hiccups.

"Please...please do not harm her."

"Her?" The captain's face lit up. "Oh my, sweetpea, scandalous indeed. Name. Now."

"Chevalier," I whispered, hating myself. "Madame Ismay Chevalier."

"Good girl," Captain Halliwell cooed. "That wasn't so hard."

I glared at her. "Do not call me that."

"Why? Is that what she called you?" she jeered.

"No!"

Despite my indignation, or perhaps because of it, the captain continued to lace her questions with cruel barbs for what felt like hours. She wanted to know everything about me. About my father's business. About Madame's tutorage. My friends and family. She seemed determined to lay me completely bare.

"What cares do you have for my daily life?" I asked exasperated. The stress of the day was taking its toll and I felt like a well-wrung sponge.

"I'm gauging how much I can ransom you for. You do indeed keep some illustrious company, which is points in your favor." The captain shrugged. "It's also useful for business to know the comings and goings of the high and mighty. They are, of course, my best customers."

"They would never deal with the likes of you."

The words were out of my mouth before I could stop them, but Captain Halliwell simply gave me a wry smile.

"Is that what you think, sweetpea? That there are only good people and pirates? Let me ask you this then, how much gold did you give to your precious lover to set up your wonderous, new life together, hm? The family jewels?"

I frowned as she chuckled. I had given Madame some valuable jewelry to help expedite our escape, but I had volunteered it. She would never betray me like that.

"If you are suggesting—"

"I'm not suggesting. I'm telling. You got scammed. She took your money and shipped you off never to be seen again. It's not exactly unheard of."

"How dare you!"

She smirked. "Believe me or don't. That's your business. We shall see how quickly a life at sea will knock some sense into you. If you even survive your punishment."

"My what?"

A sharp look had me quickly adding, "Captain."

"You don't think I've forgotten you stowed away on my ship, do you? That's a crime, sweetpea." Her face spread into a horrible, malicious grin. "Time to pay the price."

Chapter Four

I flinched as the captain reached for me, but she only gripped my collar and dragged me from my chair. She slid an arm around me to guide me on deck. We were of the same height, and I fell easily into step with her. In another life, it might have been intimate, romantic even, how she held me close. I was not fooled. Something horrible was about to happen to me and whimpers crawled up my throat with each step.

As she walked me to the center mast, the sailors around paused in their work to watch.

No, not just sailors. Pirates. Bloodthirsty, murdering pirates. Like ones from the stories that I had read and then had nightmares about as a child. The flag that flew from the mast was as black as night and a skull leered down at me from its folds, maw gaping. I would have pinched myself to make sure this was all not a bad dream had Captain Halliwell not already struck me.

"Remove your shirt."

For a moment, I thought I had misheard the captain and simply looked at her blankly.

"Take it off," she repeated with a glint of malice in her eyes, "or I'll have one of my crew assist you."

I glanced at the leering faces of the pirates that had moved in to form a circle around us and wrapped my arms around myself. I could not bare myself in front of these men. I could not. What an absurd order. I stared at her, appalled, but her iron expression did not budge.

"Please…" I whispered. Surely, she would understand. "I cannot."

The captain rolled her eyes. "Ramsden? You've met my first mate, haven't you sweetpea?"

Ramsden, it seemed, was the name of the angry man that had found me in the hold and had been so determined to throw me overboard.

I could see him much more clearly now. For a pirate, he was dressed neatly enough, a neckerchief tucked around his throat, his sideburns combed and trimmed, although they did little to distract from his twisted jaw that looked like it had been badly broken at some point.

I screamed as he grabbed for me, but I was neither fast nor strong enough to prevent him from tearing the garment from my body. The sound of fabric being shredded between his meaty fists was enough to begin my sobs anew. He jerked the tattered remains from me, even as I tried in vain to hold onto them. I bowed almost double, trying to shield myself from the sailors' gaze. No man had ever seen me bare. My heartbeat thundered in my ears, but I was vaguely aware that the captain was scolding Ramsden for ruining perfectly good clothing.

My breaths were coming fast and loud, but my lungs did not seem to be getting any air. Humiliation heated my bones just as the sea air chilled my sweat-slick skin, but it appeared I was not allowed time to dwell on my predicament. As I was pulled towards the mast and shoved against it, it dawned on me what the captain had planned and started to struggle.

"Please," I begged, my words distorted as my face pressed into the wood. "Please do not do this."

"Keep moving, and it'll be so much worse," Ramsden promised as he yanked my hands around the mast so that I held it in an awkward embrace. The wood scraped my arms and bare breasts as my ruined shirt was wound around my wrists to keep me in place.

The captain's touch was tender as she brushed wayward strands of hair from the smooth, unblemished skin of my back and shushed my pleas for mercy.

"Ten lashes," the captain announced. "I'll do it myself."

I cringed, clinging to the mast tightly as if it could save me.

I mumbled a stream of pleas and prayers against the wood as I heard her take up position. Then I simply clenched my teeth and waited for the inevitable.

The whistle and subsequent crack of the whip hitting my back was deafening in the tense silence, but it was nothing compared to the scream I let out at its bite. My knees buckled and I would have collapsed were I not so securely attached to the mast. The pain that shot through me was harsher than I ever thought possible. The most physical discomfort I was accustomed to was an improperly laced corset or my shoes rubbing after a day's promenade. Surely, this was death.

I had no chance to drag in a breath or try and get my legs to support me again before the second blow came. And then the third…the fourth…the fifth.

I was on fire when I was finally cut loose and allowed to fall to the blessedly cool deck. My throat was raw, and my ears rang from the sounds of my own screams.

"I am dead," I whispered to myself. "I am dead, and this is damnation."

"You're not dead, you pathetic creature."

I dragged my eyes open to a pair of boots in front of my face. Captain Halliwell scowled down at me.

"Get up."

"I cannot."

"Lie there then. Let the boys get a nice, good look at you."

My eyes snapped open. I had forgotten I was

exposed. I may not have expired at the end of the captain's lash, but the thought of dozens of eyes on my bare skin almost made me wish I had.

"Come," the captain barked at me.

This time, I scrambled to follow her back into her cabin, hiding as much of my nakedness as possible from the men's stares and biting back cries with every stumbled step. The privacy of the cabin was a blessed mercy, and I all but fell through the door. My back was burning, and I focused on dragging in shallow breath after breath as Captain Halliwell retrieved a small stool and set it in the middle of the floor.

"Sit. Stay."

"I am not a dog!" I blurted. Pain and anger had made me far bolder than I should have been, and I regretted the words as soon as they left my lips.

When the captain rounded on me, I quailed under her furious expression and inched my way to the stool. Once I was seated, to my surprise, the captain left. My heart still thundered in my ears but, in the stillness of the cabin, my breathing finally evened out. My thoughts scrambled over one another. I could not even begin to fathom the mess I had gotten myself into.

I could not bring myself to do anything but sit, frozen with the shock of it all, until the captain returned. She carried with her a bucket that sloshed water over the rim onto the floor.

"Stay still," she ordered, setting down the bucket.

I kept my arms crossed tightly over my chest, as if I could claw back some of my dignity as she lowered herself to her knees behind me. I risked a glance.

She dipped a ragged, old cloth into the water and pressed it to my back. I had braced myself for it to be icy cold, but the water was warm as it dripped down, soaking the back of my pants. The pleasantness of the warmth was short-lived, however. When it came into contact with broken skin from one of the more vicious lashes, I bit back a shriek and clenched my fists around the edge of the stool. Heated salt water, I realized.

The captain was surprisingly gentle as she sponged off the blood and sweat from my skin. I was used to someone else cleaning me, be it my lady's maids or Madame Chevalier when we bathed together in her apartments in a marble bath filled with exotic scents and soaps, but the captain's touch felt uncomfortably intimate as her fingertips traced the welts she had left on me. My dazed mind wondered if her softness meant that she regretted it but I quickly put that thought aside.

"It's not that bad," she said quietly.

"Not bad?" I hissed as I tried not to flinch.

The captain laughed and all trace of the softness vanished.

"I suppose for you it might feel that way. Poor little sweetpea," she crooned.

"My name is Elise," I grunted, wincing as the captain cleaned off a particularly tender spot between my shoulder blades.

"So you said, sweetpea," the captain responded with a crooked smirk as she dropped the rag into the bucket. She produced a roll of bandages and set to work, winding the fabric around my torso across the fiery lines left by the lash. "Be thankful that I made sure this will not leave scars."

She then strode to the wardrobe to retrieve a plain white shirt with wide sleeves, which she threw in my face. "Wear that for now."

I scrambled into it, wincing. As soon as I had it over my head, the captain had grasped my arm again and steered me to the corner of the cabin. I did not resist as she forced me to the floor.

"On my ship, there is a curfew. Do not move from here, and lord help you if you disturb my rest."

"You expect me to sleep on the floor?" I asked in

amazement.

The captain rooted around in a drawer for a second before dropping a patched and faded blanket into my lap.

"Would you rather sleep at the bottom of the sea?"

"No…Captain."

"Then learn to be grateful for what I give you."

Chapter Five

I tried to cry as quietly as I could, but my back was still aflame. Not one of my attempts to find comfort on the hard floor had yielded any measure of success. Even once I had cried myself to the point of exhaustion, I knew that I would never be able to sleep. Across the cabin, the captain was sleeping soundly beneath her pile of soft-looking blankets. I glared at the ratty, threadbare covering I had been tossed. I would not have given such a thing to a dog, let alone a lady. But I was no lady within these wooden walls. I was nothing but an unwanted stowaway. Tears threatened to spill once again, and I wiped my eyes with my sleeve in frustration. What would Mother say? As a matter of fact, what would I say to myself if I saw myself like this? I gave myself a vigorous mental shake. I was on a pirate ship. An honest to goodness pirate ship. I would never have this opportunity again. As the captain started to snore, I realized that I could look around without fear of being observed. I had been too terrified earlier to take in my surroundings properly.

The cabin was about the size of my father's study and mostly occupied by the captain's desk and shelves full of books and nautical instruments. The captain's bunk was across the cabin from my corner, and heavy curtains hung beside it so that the nook could be made private. Currently, however, they hung open and I could see the shadowy shape of the sleeping captain and the slow rise and fall of her breathing. Moonlight shone in from the huge paned window behind the captain's desk and bathed the room in blue light.

As I tentatively eased to my feet, I could see the black waters of the sea through the window and the small waves that crested into white tipped peaks.

The welts on my back throbbed with every move I made but I grit my teeth and told myself it was manageable. Creeping across the intricately embroidered rug that covered the bare planks of the floor, I made my way to the desk that dominated the cabin. If there was going to be something of note, then I would find it here. Captain Halliwell was neat, for a pirate that was, and the desk was arranged with stacked scrolls and strange devices all in a row. I did not have the first idea about seafaring, but I concluded that they must be for either drawing or navigating. I assumed that the dozens of rolled up sheets of parchment that stood in a barrel behind the desk were nautical maps. Common items also had their place—an inkpot and quill, an unlit candle in its holder, a filigreed letter opener. I picked up the letter opener. I knew things of value when I saw them, and this was undoubtedly the work of a fine craftsman. I wondered where the pirate captain had acquired it. Plunder from some unfortunate merchant ship, most likely.

I was about to return it and see if the shelves would offer more interesting finds when something hard pressed against the back of my head. My blood ran cold.

"Put down the knife and turn around. Slowly."

I dropped the letter opener with a gasp and spun around. Captain Halliwell pressed the pistol against my forehead.

"I said slowly," she snarled.

"Captain!" I gasped. My hands raised of their own accord as my eyes flickered from the weapon to the woman's furious face and back again. "I did not mean to wake you. I was just…I was just…"

"Looking for something to stab me with as I slept?" The captain growled, seizing me by the back of the neck.

"What? No! No, I was—"

My plea of innocence was interrupted as I was thrown to the floor. I cried out as she kicked me in the side, making me roll over onto my injured back. I bit back a scream and tried to roll away or arch up off the floor as to not put my full weight on it as hot pain lanced up my spine, but Captain Halliwell straddled me and forced me down. As she loomed over me, I saw something clenched in her fist and immediately brought my arms up to shield my face and await whatever blow was surely about to land.

The strike never came. Instead, the captain dragged my hands away from my face. She looked wild in the moonlight.

"I was far too lenient with you," she hissed.

"I am sorry! Please, I was just looking! I shall go back to the corner!"

Captain Halliwell scoffed as she pinned my hands together. I then saw what it was she had in her fist. It was a rope.

"Wait, no! Please do not bind me!" I cried as the pirate looped it around my wrists. Fighting was futile as my strength was laughable compared to hers, but I tried nonetheless, legs flailing. I may as well have laid still as all I achieved was scraping my tender back against the floorboards. Begging proved as useful as trying to fight her.

"That is far too tight!" I squealed as she yanked the knots closed.

Captain Halliwell ignored me.

When she was finished binding my hands, the captain stood and grasped them once more. Without so much as a glance, she dragged me by my wrists back to the corner of the cabin while I flailed like a fish on a hook.

"I have survived far cleverer attempts on my life from far more devious foes," she snarled as she dumped me on the floor and yanked my hands above my head. An iron ring embedded in the wall, one of many to secure furniture and loose items during rough seas, made an ideal tethering point.

"I was not—"

"Quiet!" The captain hit me. Not hard, a simple cuff about the ear, but it was enough to stun me into silence. With the quick skill of a sailor, she had the rope knotted in seconds and then crouched to look me in the eyes, taking hold of my jaw as I tried to look away.

"You are lucky that you are worth your weight in gold, otherwise I would have you off this ship and into the depths before you could blink for a stunt like that," she hissed. "Even if I accept that you are merely simple-minded—"

"I am not simple-minded!"

"—and thought rooting around in my desk to find a blade was a good idea? I do not take kindly to being woken for no reason, nor to threats. If I hear so much as a peep from you again tonight, I will make that beating you took earlier feel like a tickle. Is that clear?"

My glare faltered.

"Yes," I said finally.

"Yes, what?" The captain's nails dug into my cheeks, and I winced.

"Yes, Captain."

Chapter Six

Somehow, I managed to dose off in the early hours, exhaustion finally triumphing over discomfort, and I was roused by a curt rapping on the cabin door. I opened my eyes reluctantly and winced at the stiffness in my neck as I raised my head. My hands, still bound above me, had gone numb some time ago. I had enough slack that I had managed to twist to lean sideways rather than put any weight on my back, but it still ached. I could say with certainty that that had been the worst night's sleep of my life.

The captain sat at her desk, book in hand, reading in the morning light. She did not even spare me a glance as she called, "Enter!"

The door swung open to admit a portly woman with wiry gray hair that was cropped short. She wore a stained apron and carried a steaming tray as she stomped into the cabin.

I perked up slightly at the smell of eggs and bacon.

My father believed in a good breakfast, and our table was always heavy in the mornings. He often invited business associates to break their fast with us as opposed to tea in the afternoons or dining with us in the evening. His work often took him away from home for the majority of the day, but breakfast could always be relied upon. I met Mr. Thompson the younger for the first time at one such breakfast. It was at another I was informed that we would be wed.

"Mornin', Cap'n!" the woman brayed as she kicked the door shut behind her.

"Morning, Petra." The captain graced the woman with a smile. It was the first time I had seen her smile when it was not dripping with malice. She actually had a nice smile. It softened her face so much I actually had to look twice.

Petra stomped to the desk and set the tray down. "Just the way you like it, Cap'n. Wasn't sure if I should bring extra…" She cast around the room. The news that the captain had decided to keep the stowaway rather than slinging her off the ship had clearly made the rounds. Petra's roving eyes found me. One eyebrow rose.

I cringed, thinking how wretched I must look. My eyes were most likely red and puffy, my hair a tangled mess and I was still bound against the wall. I drew my knees up towards my chest, trying to make myself disappear.

"That will be all, Petra." The captain followed her gaze to gift me a sneer. "Little brats who try and stab people in their sleep do not get breakfast."

My heart sank. I had not eaten a thing since early the day before and my stomach had started growling. I had thought perhaps fear would have chased away my appetite, but I was ravenous. I thought longingly of my little food pack tucked away in the chest, but that was most likely in the belly of one of the pirates already.

Petra's expression hardened. "Right you are, Cap'n."

After the cook had left, Captain Halliwell ate in silence. The only sounds were the occasional rustle of her parchment as she perused various documents or the creak of floorboards as I tried to adjust my position, discomfort mounting. Eventually, I simply could not take it anymore.

"Captain?" My voice cracked and it came out as a rasp. I cleared my throat and tried again, "Captain?"

I regretted speaking at all when the captain set down her fork and shot me an icy glare.

"Please, might you unbind me? I need to…that is, I must…I have to…"

I stuttered into silence. The captain gave a heavy sigh but, to my relief, stalked over to my corner. With a few clever pulls, the rope loosened, and I hissed as blood finally returned to my extremities. To my surprise, the captain took my hands in her own and massaged from my bruised wrists to the tips of my blue-nailed fingers. She examined the chafe marks, checked that I still had movement in my joints and rubbed my skin until warmth returned. Her palms were rough, but she handled me with the same gentleness as when she had cleaned my wounds.

"What are you doing?" I asked quietly.

"You'll be worth less if your hands fall off because I was careless," the captain murmured.

"Thank you," I whispered.

The captain snorted and thrust my hands back at me. "The only reason I'm releasing you is that I don't want you to piss on my floor."

Heat flooded my cheeks at her crassness.

The captain straightened and indicated to a door that blended in so well with the wooden walls that I had not noticed it. "Be quick about it," she snapped.

The door led to a tiny space with a bench. A hole in the middle dropped away to nothing and, when I leaned over, I could see churning waves underneath. I silently swore that I would never take my privy for granted again as I did what I had to do as quickly as possible.

When I exited the horrid excuse for a latrine, I hovered awkwardly. Was I supposed to return to the corner? I balked at the idea. However much the captain may deign to treat me as such, I was not an animal.

The captain was back at her desk, scribbling away this time. A captain's log, perhaps? I would surely feature in it. I took a step closer, but before I could see what she was writing, she stopped and snapped the ledger closed.

"Come with me." Captain Halliwell spoke without

looking at me and pushed her chair back from the desk.

She strode to the door without checking that I was following. The morning was bright and cold, and the sharp sting of ocean air chased the exhaustion from my bones. Even if I had never sailed, I had always loved the thrill of the sea.

My moment of calm was shattered when the captain's fingers tightened on my arm. Fear shot through me. I was clearly not yet forgiven for my misdemeanor the night before.

"I am curious, sweetpea," Captain Halliwell began with deadly calm. "If you indeed managed to murder me in my sleep last night, what was to be your next move?"

Before I could utter a denial, she spoke again. "Imagine you have indeed just stabbed me through the heart or slit my throat, callously leaving me in a pool of my own blood, what do you do now? The door to the cabin was locked. I imagine you take the key from my still warm corpse..."

I cringed at her words, making the captain chuckle.

"So, you exit the cabin. Naturally, a ship never sleeps. The night shift are still on deck. Do you kill them too?" She peered at me, her lip curling in derision. "No, I don't think so. I think you're sneakier than that, pretending to be an innocent little lady. We'll say you somehow manage to avoid them. Now what?"

Her grip on my elbow was painful as she dragged me across the deck to the railing. The few pirates scattered around pretended to be hard at work scrubbing the deck but were watching us with barely hidden smirks.

The breath was forced from my lungs as the captain shoved me against the railing. A hand in my hair kept me bent over the side.

Before I could blubber and beg for my life again, I realized that Captain Halliwell was not forcing me over the edge but rather making me look down. Below, a single rowboat swung in a tangled hammock of ropes. I could feel the swell of her breast under her clothing as the captain's body pressed against me. The softness was jarring against the hard, casual violence of her demeanor. A hint of some sweet scent reached me under the tang of salt and sweat as she leant in close and a stray strand of her hair tickled my face. Not quite a perfume but pleasant none the less.

"There's your escape plan. Good luck trying to launch her by yourself. Without drawing attention. And then rowing for hours on end." She yanked me back with a cruel smile. "Or were you planning to swim?"

"I was not planning anything," I ground out through clenched teeth. It felt like my hair was being ripped out as I resisted her pull. "I just became curious when I could not sleep!"

"That better be the truth," the captain growled.

"Ow! It is! I swear it!"

"Oh, well if you swear it," the captain mocked, releasing my hair and causing me to trip. "I should lock you in the brig, but the rats would probably eat you alive."

She laughed at the look on my face at the mention of rats. "That is why I allow you to sleep in my cabin. You would never survive it. But make no mistake, if I glean one hint that you are more than the innocent, little fool you seem to be, then I'll lock you down there myself."

The captain turned on her booted heel and strode back towards her cabin. Without looking back, she clicked her fingers. "Come!"

Fear fought with indignation at being summoned like a wayward pet. Fear won and I slunk after the captain and reluctantly left fresh air behind to return to the cabin.

Captain Halliwell indicated that I was to sit on the floor beside her desk. I did not miss the self-satisfied look on her face as I did so without complaint.

"Can you sew?"

"I am quite skilled in embroidery," I replied

hesitantly.

"Good. You'll spend the day darning these."

I did not know where she had retrieved the canvas bag from but, when she upended it over my head, it was full of socks and other articles of clothing. Unwashed socks, from the smell of it. I shrieked my disgust and swept them off my lap.

"Must you?" I glared up at the captain, but she simply smirked that infuriating smirk of hers and handed me a needle and thread.

"If they're not darned to my standard, you'll do them all again and again until your fingers bleed."

Chapter Seven

The slow, repetitive task of sewing was meditative for a while, and I could almost forget the discomfort of the hard floor or the twinge in my back, but boredom was creeping in and the gnawing of my empty belly was becoming harder to ignore. I rarely missed a meal. All the while, the captain sat at her desk, seemingly absorbed in her maps. I had the feeling that she was more observing me than she was actually working even though she did not glance my way. She clearly did not trust me to be alone in her cabin.

I tried my best closing up holes and sewing on patches for larger rips, but some of the garments were beyond saving. The fabric was sometimes so worn that I could see through it, or the bedraggled things had become more hole than anything else. I had finished the bulk of the pile when Captain Halliwell stood from her desk and clicked her fingers to summon me. I swallowed my resentment and followed. If I ever had the chance to make her regret treating me like a dog, I would take it in a heartbeat.

We crossed the deck and down into the belly of the ship. It was dark and narrow but, when she pushed through a double swing door, I almost cried with relief when the smell of food poured out from inside.

My mouth watered as we crossed a long room filled with narrow tables and benches–obviously a crude dining hall–and into the humid kitchen at the far end.

I almost did not see Petra behind the garlands of onions that hung from the ceiling until she bellowed out a greeting to the captain.

"Ah, Grace!" she boomed, catching sight of us.

At Captain Halliwell's scowl, she saluted sheepishly instead. "Cap'n."

So, Grace was the captain's given name. I squinted at her out of the corner of my eye. I do not know what I expected her name to be, but certainly not something as pretty and elegant as Grace.

As we ventured farther into Petra's domain, I could not help but wrinkle my nose. Pools of what I hoped was some kind of sauce congealed at our feet while onion skins and peelings littered what little work surface was available. Stacks of dirty dishes rose up from the floor almost to the height of the surfaces. But as chaotic a cook as Petra seemed to be, whatever she was cooking smelled wondrous. Something deeply savory and meaty bubbled in a pot that was more a cauldron as Petra slung more vegetables into it. Behind the scent of the stew was also the unmistakable smell of baking bread. My mouth watered as I spotted a pile of fresh rolls.

I reached out for one only to have the back of my hand rapped by a wooden spoon.

"Ah, ah! You earn your keep on my ship, stowaway," the captain scolded.

"I have been sewing for hours!" I protested, rubbing my knuckles. "I thought that was why you brought me here? I have not had a bite to eat all day."

"And now you'll clean for a few more hours if you want to eat."

"Clean?" I stared in dismay at the mountain of dishes and the barrel of water she pointed at. "You cannot be serious."

The captain simply raised her eyebrows at me.

I looked back at Petra, hoping she might take pity on me, but the smile that spread over her face was not one I liked.

"I will not clean dishes!" I managed not to stomp my

foot, but outrage coursed through my veins. "I will not!"

My stubbornness quaked as Captain Halliwell stalked towards me. I backed away, my backside hitting the massive barrel of water. There was nowhere for me to run.

I was sure she was going to hit me again but instead she grabbed the back of my neck, spun me and dunked my entire head in the water. It was freezing cold and, for one utterly terrifying moment, I thought she was going to hold me under, but she released me almost immediately and I flew back from the barrel gasping and spluttering.

A chorus of raucous laughter met me as I stood there, shocked and dripping. The first shift had come in for their meal, including the brute who had so eagerly stripped me the day before. Ramsden, the captain had called him. He leered at me and licked his lips.

My wet shirt was entirely transparent and, once again, my breasts were on full display, this time with my nipples standing to attention due to the iciness of the water. I dropped to my knees and cowered behind the barrel as the sailors laughed and my face heated. I had been whipped for goodness' sake. If I could survive that then I could endure some mockery, I told myself, but it did not stop shame curling in my belly as crass comments sailed across the room. A red-haired man behind Ramsden jeered something I did not understand but, from his gestures and the way he mimed thrusting his hips, I could make a good guess.

"Shut your trap, Marcos," Captain Halliwell retorted but she still grinned along with them. "Petra, she's all yours. Let me know if she gives you any trouble. Just don't damage her."

The look she gave me was full of unspoken threats, but she did not utter a word as she swept from the kitchen.

"Enough, you dogs! Who's hungry?" The cook seemingly commanded almost as much respect as the captain, I realized as they all fell in line.

"Well, you heard her, girl." Petra nodded to the pile of crockery. "Get to it."

"I have not…" I began to wring my hands. I certainly did not want to earn myself another dunking, but I had rarely even set foot into the kitchen in our manor, let alone been expected to work there.

"I do not know how to clean dishes," I admitted finally caving under her harsh observation.

Petra's barking laugh made me flinch.

"Got ourselves a proper little lady, have we?"

Before I could answer, she steered me over to the pile.

"Water. Soap. Dishes." She pointed at each and then shoved a coarse, bristled brush into my hands. "Brush. Pick a dish, get on your knees and scrub until it's clean, then put it over there." She pointed to a rack of shelves on the opposite side of the kitchen and squeezed my shoulder. "If it's not done to my satisfaction, I'll tan your hide. Enough instruction for you?"

With that, she stomped back to her bubbling stew and stirred with an oar-like spoon. I was really going to have to do this, I realized. Water dripped from my brow as I tried to wring out my sopping hair.

The red-haired man, Marcos, yelled something crude about me being on my knees. I ignored him but quietly smiled when Petra reached over her pot to twist his ear.

"How hard can it be," I muttered to myself, picking up one of the shallow, wooden bowls. It was crusted in whatever it had last contained, and my nose wrinkled again. Holding it at arm's length, I dipped it into the water. It did not seem to make it any cleaner. I poked at the grime with the brush.

"Put some elbow grease into it!"

I startled at the shout, almost dropping the bowl. Petra rolled her eyes at me from across the room. I ground my teeth together until tears stopped pricking at my eyes. Raised voices never failed to make me feel like a child.

I tried again, cringing at the now wet remains of whatever foodstuffs clung to the bowl.

"Don't be so damn precious about it and scrub, you useless thing!"

"My name is Elise!" I yelled back.

I surprised myself with the shout. I never raised my voice. It was unladylike and unacceptable. Mother would never have stood for it. But there was something cathartic about it and it loosened some of the stiffness in my shoulders. I scrubbed until the surface of the bowl was smooth to the touch and I held it up to show Petra, triumphant.

"What are you smiling at, *Elise*?" she sneered. "All that time for one measly plate? Get back to work."

My pride withered and died.

From then on, the two of us worked mostly in silence—her either cooking or serving up steaming bowls as each shift appeared and me cleaning—even though I was sure I heard her laugh at me when one of the large pots slipped from my grasp into the water barrel, the resulting splash soaking me to the skin yet again. The saltwater stung tiny cuts on my hands, and my back flared into pain whenever I bent in any direction. My muscles were aching from exertion within no time but, when I tried to take a moment's rest, my ever-present overseer was quick to remind me that resting was not part of my task.

When the rumbling of footsteps announced the arrival of more hungry crew members, I naively thought I might be getting dinner along with them this time. Petra took one look at my hopeful face and laughed outright, adding more utensils to my pile of work.

After the sailors finished their meal with much hollering and braying, the stack grew even taller.

I could not keep up and my frustration was mounting.

My fingertips were a wrinkled mess. I was tired. I was hungry. Dizziness threatened to fell me as I lifted the latest stack of bowls. As I caught onto the wall to steady myself, they clattered to the floor.

"Useless," Petra muttered loud enough for me to hear.

"I am not!" I yelled, my temper bubbling over. "I am plenty useful! Just not with menial servant work!"

"Watch your mouth," the cook growled. Then something that almost looked like pity crossed her features. "Go sit. The rest are all done."

I groaned as I eased my weary body onto one of the benches. Exhausted, filthy, wet and hungrier than I had ever been, when Petra finally thrust a bowl of stew into my hands, I dug in gracelessly, shoveling chunks of potato into my mouth. If Mother could see me now, I thought mirthlessly, that would be just about the only thing that could make this worse.

Chapter Eight

When Petra finally escorted me back to the captain's quarters, I slunk to the corner unprompted. Throwing the meagre covering I had been given over myself, I curled up with my face to the wall. If the captain noticed my misery, she seemingly did not care. She was engrossed in a book and her head had not even lifted once except when she offered a grunt of acknowledgement to the cook. I would never have thought pirates were the studious type, but the captain seemed an avid reader.

I had hoped that her book was interesting enough for her to leave me alone, but alas it was not. When her presence loomed behind me, I refused to look.

"Sweetpea."

I squeezed my eyes shut. Responding to the ridiculous name was the last thing I wanted to do, but I did not have it in me to fight this battle. I was done. She had been right. It had not even taken two days to break me.

"Can you not leave me alone?" I asked in a whisper, clutching my blanket. "Have I not done enough?"

"Worn out already?" The captain chuckled.

"Please, Captain. Just let me sleep."

"You'll sleep when I allow it. Up with you."

A sharp kick was delivered to my shins when I did not move fast enough for her liking. "Up!"

"I am up, you beast!" I cried, rubbing my leg. I would be nothing but a mass of bruises in the morning.

Her smirk was infuriating.

"I'm going to pretend I did not hear that, sweetpea. Come! Time to write your ransom letter."

She sounded entirely too cheerful about it. I supposed it made sense that the prospect of gold made a pirate happy. I sat on the stool beside her desk as she indicated while she set out parchment and ink on the desk before me.

"I will dictate and you will write."

"Yes, Captain," I grumbled.

"Dear Father, I find myself in unfortunate circumstances..." Captain Halliwell began.

I dutifully put ink to parchment.

"I have been naïve and foolish enough to trespass aboard a ship…"

I shot her a glare. "I would never write that. Is this letter not supposed to be from me?"

"You will write what I tell you to."

"Why do you not write it yourself?" I snapped, slamming the quill down.

"Silence, or I will find something to shove in that pretty mouth of yours." The captain's eyes sparkled, and I had no doubt that she would go through with her threat if I continued to argue. "Pick up the quill."

I fumed but did indeed pick up the quill and silently wrote the rest of her ridiculous letter while grinding my teeth until we got to the part about her compensation.

"In exchange for my care and subsequent safe return home, the merciful captain is requesting compensation of ten thousand pounds…"

"You cannot be serious!" I blurted upon hearing the amount she intended to demand for me.

"Deadly serious."

"That is an absurd amount!"

"And just how much is your dowry for your upcoming nuptials?"

"That…" I blustered. "That is an entirely different

thing! My father will never agree to this!"

"I can be very persuasive."

"This letter will not convince him," I said, shoving the parchment away.

"You'd better hope it does, because you will not like my second letter."

The look on her face made me squirm as foreboding crept up my spine. "Why?"

She moved like lightning, reaching across to seize my wrist and yanking me halfway across the desk.

"What are you doing?" I shrieked.

"You're still dreadfully slow, sweetpea."

The edge of the desk dug into my stomach. I tried to pull my hand back, but she held me where she wanted me.

She took my thumb between her fingers and wiggled it. "This little piggy went to market."

"I am not a child!" I spat, trying to wrestle my hand back. I hated how she toyed with me. How she looked at me like I was something to eat. How her shirt gaped open as she leant forward over the desk and I could not stop the way my pulse raced at the tantalizing view.

She moved to the next finger and then the next. "This little piggy stayed home…this little piggy had roast beef…and this little piggy had none…"

"And this little piggy…" She grinned as she reached my little finger and drew a dagger from her belt. I froze, my eyes stretching wide as she pressed the tip to the base of my finger. "This little piggy is going to go oink, oink, oink all the way back to your father as a little incentive if he refuses my initial demands."

She released me suddenly and I flew backwards, toppling my stool and landing hard on her luxurious rug. I clutched my hand to my chest as she threw back her head and laughed.

"Let's hope it doesn't come to that hm, sweetpea?

Now be a good girl and start again. You spilled ink all over your letter."

I did not think I had ever truly hated anyone more when she winked at me. I glared at her but kept my mouth shut as I rewrote the letter as neatly, and as convincingly, as I could. The captain seemed satisfied by my renewed efforts and clicked her tongue approvingly as she inspected my work.

I swallowed hard. Did she truly need to stand so close to me? I flinched as her hands came to my shoulders and she gave a light squeeze.

"How is your back?" she murmured, lifting the back of my shirt and nudging me forward so that she could look.

"Are you worried that you have reduced my value?" I spat.

I kept my eyes on the edge of the desk as she removed the bandages and her fingertips traced the marks she had left on me.

"It will not hurt much longer, I think."

There it was again. That tinge of regret in her voice. I twisted round so that I could see her face, but her stony expression was firmly in place.

"Do not pretend that you care."

The captain chuckled. "I simply do not like damaging pretty things. But I will if I have to."

Her eyes bored into mine and my thoughts tumbled over themselves as I tried to process her threat alongside the fact that she found me pretty. I was too exhausted, too drained and my emotions were running riot, that was all. I did not care what she thought of me. She was the worst person I ever had the misfortune to meet.

The captain stepped away and fluttered her hand at me.

"Now you may sleep. Go. And don't you dare think of moving from that corner. I have plenty more rope."

I swallowed my angry reply. I was bone-tired and all

I wanted was to lie down, sleep and escape this nightmare for a few hours at least. Provoking the captain was not a clever thing to do, but she made my blood boil and it took effort to force down my feelings.

My blanket brought me little comfort as a covering but, with it rolled up into a makeshift pillow, I settled myself as comfortably as I was able.

Captain Halliwell was turning in for the night too.

I peeked over my shoulder. Her coat was already hanging on a hook next to her bunk as she stripped off her shirt too. My breath caught. Her back and shoulder muscles were pulled taut as she stretched. I had never thought a woman could have such a body. Such strength. Hard muscle but soft lines. Tapering to her waist. Her hips. Candlelight flickered across her skin as she hung her shirt on the hook next to her coat. I caught sight of the gentle curve of a breast as she turned ever so slightly. She took her time, as if she were displaying herself for me. She terrified me and I hated her but, oh I would love to paint her. I would paint her in all the shades of gold. From the shining, sun-bleached highlights in her hair and the candlelight flickering across her skin to the deep, dark shadows of her eyes.

I let my gaze rove once more over her body and, when I lifted it again, I saw those dark eyes were fixed on me, an amused smile played across her full lips. I squeaked and hid my face with my blanket. I did not emerge until I had heard her blow out the last candle and settle in her bunk.

She had already dragged the truth from me that my preference was for women. I would rather die than let her think I would ever come close to viewing her in that way.

Chapter Nine

I awoke groggy and disoriented as if surfacing from quicksand that was determined to hold me under. The morning sunlight streamed into the cabin, making me blink as it stabbed at my eyes. Despite my discomfort, sleep had come for me almost immediately, but I still did not feel rested. I eased myself up into a sitting position, my muscles aching, to see the captain at her desk, quill in one hand and a glint of gold in the other. She was murmuring to herself as she flipped a coin between her fingers. I could not help but listen in.

"Twenty percent of seven hundred and forty..." she muttered under her breath. "...is one hundred and...no....is one hundred and..."

Her forehead was furrowed in concentration and her lips moved now silently as she fought with the numbers.

"One hundred and forty-eight," I said after a moment.

Captain Halliwell flinched. She had not noticed I was awake.

"What did you say?"

"Twenty percent? The answer is one hundred and forty-eight."

The captain looked over her notes and then up at me. "You did that in your head?"

I shrugged. "I used to like to be in my father's office while he did his accounts when I was younger. It was the only time I got to spend with him. I would sit on the rug in front of the fire with my dolls or a book, hoping that he would call me over. When he occasionally did, I would clamber into his lap. 'Look at this,' he would say. 'What do you see?' And I would respond with something like 'numbers, father?' and then as I got a little older, I could reply 'purchasing orders, father' or 'interest rates, father'."

I was babbling again but Captain Halliwell did not seem inclined to stop me. She watched with rapt attention and a raised eyebrow as I continued to let the words pour out. Perhaps if she saw me as more of a person she would be more inclined to treat me as such, I reasoned.

"He would point out some small detail or other that had made him money or given him leverage. I was always so proud and happy for him. I loved sitting with him and learning about his company and how it all worked. I thought I might join him properly one day but—"

I caught myself and swallowed. I had been about to share too much.

It seemed the more I learned about my father's business, the less he shared. Once, I made a recommendation to my father. Only once. I could no longer recall what it was I had said, only the manner in which he looked at me. I thought he would be pleased, proud even, but it was as if a shadow passed over him and he told me curtly that I should leave. The next day when I tried to go and sit in his office with him, I found the door locked. I was informed that I should give my father privacy and not distract him from his important work anymore.

It was after that I threw myself into my painting. It seemed that the only time I was ever allowed to express myself would be through my art. I supposed it was fitting for a lady—beautiful to look at but, most importantly, silent. My father had always enjoyed my landscapes, so I painted a dozen, hoping to salvage some of his affection but he simply nodded his acceptance. The last time I caught a glimpse of his office, one was hanging behind his desk.

"Anyway," I stammered, "I learned enough to be quite good with numbers."

"Well, well, well." The captain's shark eyes looked me up and down with a glint of amusement. "Maybe there is some use to you after all."

My annoyance must have shown on my face because she laughed. "We shall pick this up later. Petra's waiting for you in the galley. I trust you can make it there without getting into trouble."

"I am to clean again?" I asked in dismay. "I thought my punishment was over?"

The captain laughed again but, this time, it was a sharp bark.

"Earning your keep isn't punishment. Well, I suppose it is for someone who's never worked a day in her life. On the Bone Heart, you work for your supper."

She shuffled her papers and, when I still had not moved, she gave me an icy glare. "I gave you an order, stowaway."

"I could help with the numbers," I offered, desperate to avoid another day's labor. "I could—"

"You are testing my patience, sweetpea," she growled. "Go. Now."

"But—"

The captain slammed her hand on the desk, making me flinch.

"So help me God, one more word out of you…" She pointed a menacing finger at me but, before she could finish whatever threat she was going to make, I had fled the cabin.

I thought about staying on deck for a while, but I would only be postponing the inevitable and earning myself more punishment. Reluctantly, I made my way to the galley.

Petra met my tentative "good morning" with a grunt.

I peered past her to the water barrel to see that it was already occupied. A boy of maybe fifteen with rumpled, sandy hair and limbs that seemed to long for him was already slinging plates into the water.

"The captain sent me to assist you again." I shot a confused look at the boy who was now elbow-deep in soapy water. "Am I not to clean?"

"If I had the time to wait for you to whine about it then you would be. Sully, show her to the goats and give her a shovel. Be quick about it."

"Goats?" I echoed in disbelief.

Sully, the lanky youth, rolled his eyes and wiped his wet hands on his vest. He strode to the far end of the kitchen, snatched a bucket from the corner and then shimmied down a ladder that was hidden in the corner. He did not wait for me to follow but a snarl from Petra had me scurrying after him. I lowered myself down into the gloom below, feeling for each rung before putting my weight on it. From what I had seen of the ship, it seemed in decent repair but that did not mean I did not long for the solidity and assurance of stone and mortar under my feet as I descended into the darkness. I cringed as the ladder creaked.

"Whenever you're ready, Your Highness." Sully's voice dripped in sarcasm.

I shot him a glare as I reached the bottom of the ladder. He laughed and strode off down a narrow corridor without a backwards glance.

I had assumed that when Petra said goats that it was some sort of pirate code but, the farther we went down into the bowels of the ship, the smell made it clear that it was not.

"Why on earth are there goats on a ship?" I asked Sully, slightly out of breath from following his long-legged strides.

"Fresh milk. Easier than cows." He winked at me. "Then fresh meat when there's no milk left."

The smell was by now beyond pungent, and I struggled to breathe without coughing. I had my shirt up over my nose and mouth, but it did little to reduce the stench.

The end of the corridor opened up into a larger space containing animal pens. The wooden walls came up to my hip, and I could hear the braying from within as the goats realized they had company.

"Give them a bale of hay and these scraps—" He pushed the bucket full of peelings that had strewn the kitchen yesterday, into my arms "— then shovel out the shit into the pail over there and sling it down that hatch. Have fun."

I glanced between him and the pen. Six sets of slitted eyes stared back. One huge, gray beast in particular glared at me with nothing short of malice.

"Wait! Don't leave! Will you not help me?" I was wringing my hands now. Dishes were bad. This was worse.

"I've got work to do." He sniggered. "And so do you. You're at the bottom of the food chain around here. Get used to it."

He deliberately bumped my shoulder as he passed.

"Am I to be a farmhand now?" I demanded.

"Figure it out!" he called over his shoulder, still laughing.

I twisted the hem of my shirt in my hands. How much trouble would I be in if I refused to do this? Too much. Could I get away with pretending I did? No, I realized looking at the mess in the pen. The evidence would still be scattered across the floor in steaming piles.

"Argh!" This time I did stamp my foot, and several of the goats skittered back.

I pressed the heels of my hands against my eyes to stop the tears of frustration. I was going to have to toughen up if I was going to get through this. This would be nothing more than a memory soon. An amusing story to tell over after-dinner drinks in the parlor. I would wear a newly tailored dress and thrill my guests with tales of my adventure. The thought strengthened me, and I managed to calm myself. I could do this. I just had to get my bearings.

A bale of hay thrown into the pen along with the vegetable scraps was enough to distract the beasts and keep them away from me as I entered the pen, trying not to step in any of the nastiness, and inspected the hatch I was to use to dispose of their leavings. It was a simple enough job when I broke it down into steps. I had the tools I needed and, however horrible the task, it was doable.

I distracted myself with the thoughts of the dress I would buy upon my return. Blue, I decided. I would match it with the sapphire earrings I had been gifted on my twenty-first birthday. I could wear it to the new theatre that had opened recently in town. I frowned. If I was not in too much disgrace when I returned, that was.

Perhaps Mr. Thompson would withdraw his proposal. It was not unheard of, but it would bring scandal down upon my family. I tried to summon all that I knew of the man to guess where his thoughts would lie.

If I was honest with myself, the most time I had ever spent with him was on the morning he requested my hand, and I was too busy battling my own feelings to pay him much attention at all. I supposed he was handsome in his own way— fashionably clean shaven, lean and square jawed. Certainly, he could have provided for me. If I knew where I was going to end up, perhaps I would have done what my parents wanted and just gone along with it. As Mrs. Thompson, I certainly would never have had to clean out a goat pen.

A few hours later, I took back everything I ever thought about this job being easy. It was sweltering. Hotter than the kitchens even and the leavings were far heavier than I had expected. The pitchfork I had found was unwieldy and did nothing to help my balance. The goats brayed at me mockingly the whole time and tried to chew on my sleeves when they had their fill of the kitchen scraps. I no longer tried to avoid stepping in the muck. I had slipped and fallen in it twice already, and any hopes I had of remaining clean were long gone. My pants were crusted in filth, and I did not even want to look at my fingernails.

The sounds of my sniffling and the goats' constant cries were interrupted by voices from somewhere close. I perked up, hoping someone was coming to relieve me of this awful task. I should have learned that hope had no place on the Bone Heart.

Sully had returned, but he was not alone. Marcos, the red-haired pirate with the vulgar language, strolled up to the pen.

At the sight of me, pink-faced and covered in straw and goat droppings, Marcos erupted into laughter. He slapped his thighs, still laughing, and came to rest his elbows on the low wall of the pen.

"Well, well, well."

I ignored him and tried to stab at another pile.

"Don't seem like much of a lady now, do you?" he crowed. "I suppose since the captain's made you her new pet, this is the perfect place for you."

He reached in and slapped the huge gray goat on the rump. The beast shrieked and charged at the only enemy he could perceive. Me.

I tried to put my hands up, to slow him, to calm him. I do not know what my plan was, but the goat rammed me all the same. His stubby horns slammed into my belly, and I was launched back against the pen. I collapsed to the ground, curled in on myself, clutching my stomach and gasping for air.

Marcos' renewed laughter echoed off the wooden walls and faded as he sauntered back in the direction of the kitchens.

Sully stared down at me sprawled in the hay for a moment. I could see the indecision in his face and wondered if he was thinking about helping me up.

"Petra says to go get cleaned up and then help dish up lunch," he stammered before he scampered after Marcos, leaving me in the filth.

It took me a good ten minutes to stand up again and, when I did, I was alone. Except for the blasted creatures, of course. The huge, gray beast stared at me with remorseless, blank eyes.

"I hope they roast you first," I hissed at him and then escaped the pen before he could decide to charge at me again. I would beg to do dishes before coming within ten feet of that thing again, I decided as I hauled myself back upstairs.

When I returned to the captain's cabin to clean myself up as requested, the captain took one look at me and burst out laughing. I felt my temper rising. I had had quite enough of being laughed at for one day.

"Do not laugh!"

That made her laugh harder. "You were supposed to clean up after them not roll around with them!"

"Stop it!"

"Mind your manners," the captain reminded me, but her eyes were still crinkled up in mirth. "Do not step on the carpet! You'll get it as filthy as you are. Come here."

She ushered me away from anything fabric and looked me up and down.

"Get those clothes off. Everything." The captain's nose wrinkled at me as she turned to find me something else to wear.

I peeled off my filthy garments and scrubbed at my arms and face with a damp washcloth. It was not nearly sufficient.

"Can I not bathe properly?" I whined. "I need a bath."

"I'm not wasting resources on a stowaway. You're lucky I'm giving you a change of clothes."

"Have fun sharing the cabin with me then," I retorted.

That gave her pause and she sighed.

"You do stink," she huffed before fetching me a bar of hard soap. I still had to make do with cold water and a cloth instead of a proper bath but at least it was something.

"Thank you, I suppose."

I kept one arm over my bare chest as I took the soap from her. It smelled like citrus and something I could not identify. It smelled like her, I realized. I brought the bar to my nose and inhaled the sweet, spicy perfume.

"I like this scent," I murmured as I lathered it up in my hands. "What is it?"

"It's... What is that?" the captain asked sharply.

"Hm?" I followed her line of sight to my stomach where a bruise was already forming.

"Oh. It is nothing," I muttered. "One of the goats charged at me."

She caught me by the wrist before I could turn away and hide myself. Her fingertips traced over the marks. My breath caught in my throat. She was so close to me I could have counted each and every one of her long eyelashes as her eyes travelled up from my bruise, raking across my breasts that were barely hidden by my loose hair, to meet my eyes. Heat shot straight to my core at the flash of hunger I saw in them.

Of all the things I expected her to feel for me, desire was not one of them. She had said I was pretty the night before. In an indirect way, of course, and muddled in with a threat but... Captain Halliwell could not want me, could she? Before I could formulate my tangled thoughts, her sneer was back, making me wonder if I had simply imagined it.

"What did you do to annoy it?"

"'I' did not do a thing," I shot back as I jerked my wrist from her grip and stepped away from her. I must have been imagining things. That flash of desire was nothing more than my own stressed mind playing cruel tricks on me. The captain hated me, and I would do well to remember it.

Her eyes darkened. "What do you mean by that?"

"Nothing, Captain."

I may have been naïve, but I was not quite so clueless that I would risk retribution by complaining to the captain about Marcos' actions.

"I made my orders clear that you weren't to be damaged. If someone disobeyed that order, then I need to know."

"I am fine."

"I don't care how you feel. I care that you could've been hurt."

My eyebrows shot up at her statement. "You do?"

She scoffed.

"If you do not get home in one piece, sweetpea, then I do not get my gold."

"You beat me," I reminded her with a glare. "And you make me sleep on the floor like an animal. You are hardly being gentle with me. You were going to cut my finger off for goodness' sake!"

"I wasn't really going to cut it off." She rolled her eyes. "Not yet anyway. And this is gentle, sweetpea. If one of the lads had taken the whip to you, they would have peeled the flesh off your bones. I barely broke the skin. As for where you sleep, you sleep in the safety of my cabin. Be grateful for my mercy."

"If this is your idea of mercy, I would hate to know what your idea of cruelty is."

She stepped in close. So close that I could feel her warmth on my bare skin and smell the lemony scent we now shared.

"Pray that you won't have to find out."

Chapter Ten

The following day, I was allowed a small respite to stay on deck and enjoy some fresh air after a morning of scrubbing pots and kitchen surfaces until they shone. The salt spray clung to my hair in glittering beads as I stood next to the railing, watching sea birds swooping low over the water. Every now and again, one darted under the waves to emerge victorious with a thrashing silver tail disappearing down its gullet.

Behind me, the pirate with the bandana and gold medallion was lounging in a nest of tangled ropes and strumming what looked like a homemade instrument. The tune was light and melodic and, when he started to sing along, his voice was deep and soothing. I had learned that he went by the name Raul. No one had bothered to introduce themselves to me, of course, but I overheard various names as the crew ate their meals.

I sighed, closing my eyes and tipping my head back to let the sun warm my cheeks. Back home, ladies avoided the sun, but I found it pleasant. If my time at sea could continue like this, I may have a chance at surviving it.

"Not spending the day with your new goat friends? Old Billy seemed to take a fancy to you, that's for sure."

Behind Marcos, his cronies snorted. The goat story seemed to have made the rounds already.

I gripped the railing hard. Petra had told me to take a break and not bother her for an hour so I had nowhere else to flee to escape the mockery that was surely about to occur. I straightened my spine.

"Leave me be."

"Where's the fun in that?"

I kept my eyes on the waves as he sauntered over to the railing beside me. "You wouldn't say no to a little fun, would you?"

I grit my teeth and tried to push off the railing to make my escape but he caught my elbow and spun me so that my back pressed against it.

"I said, leave me be!" I hissed, my voice sounding far more confident than I felt as he crowded me.

I caught a glimpse of red velvet behind him. A heartbeat later, Captain Halliwell was at my side, glaring daggers at the pirate. She was considerably shorter than him but, as soon as she appeared, Marcos' friends melted back into the scenery, leaving him alone with her wrath.

"What do you think you are doing?" Her tone was mild, but I could feel the danger coursing from her in waves. "I said she was off limits."

"It was just a joke, Captain." Marcos laughed, looking around for support that was nowhere to be found.

"You put your hands on her."

The pirate scoffed. "She ain't hurt."

I had tried to edge away, but the captain seized my arm and wrenched up my shirt, showing off the now purple marks from the goat's horns on my soft flesh.

"I suppose this was just a joke too?" she asked.

His eyes widened at the bruises.

"That was the goat, that wasn't me. I didn't touch her."

"Do you think I'm stupid? Is that it? I distinctly remember giving the order that the stowaway was not to be harmed in any way."

I swallowed hard. On one hand, the captain was defending me. Her standing between me and Marcos, protecting me, filled my stomach with butterflies. On the other, her grip on my arm was about to give me a whole new set of bruises.

"I'm sorry, captain." The man's apology came out as a growl. "Didn't mean anything by it."

"Double duty," Captain Halliwell snarled back through her teeth. "And your rations today are forfeit. If I hear of you bothering her again, it'll be a lashing for you. Is that understood?"

"Aye, Captain," he said. He stared as his boots, but his fists were clenched.

"Get out of my sight." She gave him a filthy look and then raised her voice to the rest of the crew on deck. "Is that clear? No one is to fucking touch her!"

A chorus of "aye, Captain" sounded from across the deck. I wondered if I imagined the tinge of hostility muddled in with the voices. Marcos' cronies most likely.

Marcos himself all but sprinted away, leaving me standing alone with the captain. She seemed to realize she was still holding on to me and loosened her grip. She frowned, pausing to readjust my shirt where she had rumpled it. It was oddly tender how she fussed at my clothing, but when she caught my eye, she snatched her hands away.

"Thank you," I murmured. "For defending me."

She grunted, turning away from me.

"This is my ship. My word is law. I cannot afford to allow even a sliver of disrespect."

I had noticed before how young she was to be a captain— I now doubted she was yet thirty—but it was starkly evident as doubt flickered across her features that she was not as in control as she would like to be. I studied her profile as she looked out across the waves. A wisp of her hair fluttered across her face in the breeze, drawing my attention to her strong jaw. Those full lips.

I pinched myself. She was a murderous pirate. I could

not risk forgetting that just because she was beautiful and protected me.

I wondered how long she had been captain for. If she was worried about maintaining their respect and loyalty, then maybe not for very long. What had happened to the previous captain? A chill ran through me. Had she killed him? Is that not what pirates did? Is that not what she would have done with me if I had not been worth her while?

"Don't you have work to be getting on with?" she asked without looking at me.

"Petra said I had an hour to myself. I just wanted some air." I shifted my weight on my feet awkwardly. "I can leave if you would like."

She shrugged and I took that as acceptance of my company.

"May I ask a question?"

"If you must."

"How did you become captain?"

She turned her gaze on me, something predatory lurking beneath the surface. "Why? You think I'm not up to the job?"

"No! Not at all! I was merely wondering how it came about." I was correct about that being a touchy subject. "I was not aware that women could earn the title of captain."

Her shoulders relaxed.

"They can't on navy ships or merchant vessels, fishing boats, passenger ships. I doubt a woman would be allowed to captain a rowing boat in Beauris." She ticked them off on her fingers before giving me a crooked smile. "This is a pirate ship, sweetpea. The regular rules don't apply."

"So how did you become captain?" I pressed.

"Blood and determination."

"Give me a real answer." I jutted my chin out but still added a belated "captain" to my demand, which seemed to amuse her.

"Very well." Her lips curved up into a smile. "Like you, I had a tutor. Only, I didn't go to bed with mine."

My cheeks heated to a blaze.

"Are you capable of having a conversation without mocking me?"

"I am merely stating the facts," she replied but her grin told the truth. She was enjoying goading me.

"Maybe you are jealous that I have someone."

"Ah, yes. The lover that stole your money and abandoned you to the mercy of pirates."

"She did not!"

"You are just adorable when you're angry, sweetpea."

I let out a scream of frustration and stomped away from her. I might not be welcome back in the kitchen just yet, but that did not mean I had to be anywhere near her". I sulked on the opposite side of the deck for the remainder of my precious hour. I could no longer hear Raul's lovely music, but I was at least free of the captain's ridicule.

I went about my work in the kitchen in sullen silence and hoped the captain felt me ignoring her when I returned to the cabin that evening. I ignored her with every ounce of my being, even when I felt her eyes on me. I would sleep there if I must, but I did not have to suffer her taunts.

The captain spent most of her time on deck with the crew now that she seemed comfortable leaving me alone as long as Petra was satisfied with me. I successfully ignored her for two more days until she woke me in her usual brusque manner by nudging me awake with the toe of her boot.

I groaned and tried to roll farther away, but she was having none of it and ripped my blanket from my grasp.

"Get up. That's an order."

" Yes, captain," I replied, not bothering to hide my pout as I uncurled. It felt like I had only just managed to drift off.

"I have work for you today. There are boots to polish and breeches to patch. Get to it."

She stalked out of the cabin.

I decided to start with patching the breeches. I had never polished anything, and the last thing I needed was to accidentally ruin the captain's boots. Just like her velvet coat, they were high quality and well made. Captain Halliwell clearly had a taste for luxury. I could only imagine how she would look in a proper gown. When she shed her customary scowl, she was truly beautiful. Not to mention that in sharing a cabin with her, I had often seen the exquisite body she hid under her untailored clothing. With the right seamstress, the captain would be a sight to behold.

I shook my head, dragging myself out of ridiculous fantasies. Whatever she may look like, I reminded myself, Captain Halliwell was a brute and a pirate.

The stitching was quick work. I had always had nimble fingers. The boots, however, stared me down from across the cabin. I dared not touch them. I had a peek in the polish tin. It seemed far too little to cover the surface of the boots with, which had been my tentative plan. Was I supposed to mix it with water like I would with my paints? I had no idea.

I smudged a little of the polish on my finger and rubbed it with the pad of my thumb. It was a deep, rich brown. I snatched a piece of parchment from the captain's desk and smeared the polish on a corner. It was exactly the right color. Perfect for the image I had in my head that was begging to be let out onto the page. I bit my lip. I doubted I could have stopped myself if I had wanted to.

The captain had an assortment of quills and fine brushes for lettering, and I helped myself to one of the latter. I did not have my usual easel, so I cleared a space on the desk, careful not to move her belongings around too much. A thrill of fear shot through my veins at the thought of the captain finding me touching her things again. She would not return for hours, I told myself. She told me I would be here for the whole day, which suggested that she would not. She sent me away if she was occupying the cabin. Even as I told myself I would be safe, it was all excuses. I just wanted to paint.

I mixed the polish with a little water in the lid of the tin, just like I would with my own materials, and when I touched brush to parchment, peace washed over me. It did not matter that I was hundreds of miles from my parents' house, possibly even farther from my lover, this was home to me. Every stroke of the brush loosened the tension in my neck. I was limited to browns, but one color can be a rainbow in the right hands. In my hands. I picked out shadow in thick streaks of polish. The highlights I daubed at with my fingertips to let the paleness of the parchment shine through. This was what I loved. And I truly believed it loved me back. How else could I create beautiful things?

"Sweetpea."

I screamed.

I had been so lost in my art that the time had slipped away from me. It always did. I could lose hours.

"What is this?"

I snatched for the parchment, but Captain Halliwell was quicker.

Her eyebrow rose as she took in the portrait.

"This is what you've been doing all day?" She brandished my painting at me.

Two sets of shark eyes bored into me. I had to admit, I had done well. The likeness was striking and, in the right light, the brown could have been gold.

"I...I..."

"You painted me?"

She looked back at the portrait and cocked her head. I felt sure she was going to rip it up, and the thought had my insides twisting. It may have been crude and rough, but it was beautiful.

"Please do not tear it!" I blurted.

"Tear it? Why would I do that?" Her lips curved into a smile. "I actually quite like it."

"You…like it?"

"You're full of surprises, aren't you, sweetpea? When you said you were going to bed with your art tutor instead of painting, I took that to mean you weren't any good."

Embarrassment warred with pride in my chest and words failed me.

"I might have to sit for you to paint me a proper portrait." She nodded decisively.

"You really like it?" I repeated. A warm fluttery feeling had started up in my gut. I could not help the hopeful smile that spread across my face.

"Don't get cocky, but aye." She winked at me. "You made me look fearsome. Quite a talent you have there."

She picked up the letter opener that had caught my attention on my disastrous first night in her cabin. Twirling it in her hand, she walked to the wall and skewered my portrait with the knife before standing back to admire it with her hands on her hips.

"Oh, and sweetpea?" My face flushed as she bent to cup my cheek. My heart forgot how to beat as her thumb traced my lower lip. "If, after I let you go, I find any wanted posters with my face on them? I will hunt you down and make you regret it."

…

The skies outside had long since darkened as I lay on the hard floor, my ratty blanket clutched under my chin. Usually, I was dead to the world until morning with the amount of physical labor my poor body was being subjected to. Something had woken me. I let my eyes adjust to the darkness and pricked my ears. The wood around me creaked and wind whistled through the cracks. I could hear the waves lapping at the sides of the hull, slow and rhythmic. I glanced over at the captain's bunk, expecting to see the vague outline of her sleeping form. What I did see made my breath catch in my throat.

She was indeed lying in her bunk with her eyes closed but she was not sleeping. A shard of moonlight illuminated the smooth lines of her throat as her head tipped back even farther into her pillow. Her blanket was bunched around her waist, and one hand was hidden underneath. Her hand moved in rhythm with the lull of the sea. Heat flooded my cheeks and my belly. I should not have seen this. But I could not look away. I could hear her breathing now. Her movements caused the blanket to slip, and I could see clearly that her hand was buried in between her thighs.

Her hair was a mess, her clothes rumpled, her breathing erratic gasps. She was lost to the pleasure, and it was the most erotic thing I had ever seen. Her hips jerked, humping upwards as she pleasured herself with her hand.

My own fingers had started sliding down my body, instinctively seeking to relieve the desire that had sprung up between my own legs. I forced myself to stop. I could not move, could not let her know I was awake…that I had seen. That I was still seeing. Shamelessly watching. My lips parted as her free hand trailed up her stomach to her breast. Her shirt was unbuttoned to the navel, and I caught a glimpse of one dark nipple as she kneaded and squeezed the soft flesh. It was impossible not to imagine how it would feel under my own hands. The softness of her breasts with the hardness of her taut muscles. I would take them in my hands and then in my mouth, my tongue questing over the stiff peaks of her nipples. Her hips would be bucking into me rather than her own hand.

Lord, I wanted that. I wanted to touch. To taste. To be touched. What would she do if I climbed into bed with her? She had tied me up and threatened to beat me for disturbing her sleep, what would she do if I disturbed her now? Lust was clouding my thoughts. I do not think I would even mind if she tied me up again, if she tied me to her bed. Then she could drive those fingers into me instead.

Desire flooded through me.

I could not take it anymore. The heat between my legs was an aching, pulsing need. I shifted ever so slightly so that I could still watch her as I slid my own hand to my pants. My desperate fingers skimmed over the slickness they found there. Lord, had I ever been this wet? A guttural moan from the captain's bunk sent another shock of tingling arousal straight through me. I bit down on the corner of my blanket to stop myself from making a sound as my fingertips circled my sensitive bud. My gaze was fixed upon the captain. She was so close to coming undone. The sounds she was making were music to my ears and fuel to the fire building under my fingers as I rubbed myself. Tendons strained in her neck as she threw her head back and her body went rigid, her mouth wide open in a silent scream of ecstasy as waves of pleasure coursed through her. Another moan left her as she relaxed into the ripples of bliss. That last soft moan tipped me over the edge. Such a pure and gentle sound. My teeth clenched around my blanket as I climaxed, trying to swallow my cries as I gave myself over to the sensation. Tears sprang to my eyes as my release washed over me, leaving me a hot, quivering mess. Oh, I had needed this more than I realized.

As the pleasure ebbed away leaving a deliciously warm glow in my limbs, I glanced back over to the captain, expecting to see her sprawled in a beautiful, post-orgasmic bliss. She was not. She was propped up on her elbows and her dark eyes were open and fixed on me. I felt the blood drain from my face. I dared not breathe for what felt like several minutes. She was going to kill me for seeing her private moment, I was sure of it. She was going to storm over to where I lay with my fingers still nestled in my soaking wet folds and she was going to gut me.

I was almost convinced that my heart was going to

fail right there and then, but she simply raised one eyebrow and then rolled over to face the wall with a low chuckle.

The morning brought with it shame, awkwardness and guilt. I wanted nothing more than to stay hidden under my blanket, but that would mean admitting that the night before had actually happened, and I was adamant that I would go to my deathbed before I admitted my voyeurism to any living soul. The captain at least seemed happy enough to pretend, and she barked at me to get my ass to the kitchen in her usual abrasive tone. I could not believe I had fantasized about her.

That was also where the shame and guilt came in. How could I be thinking of other women, let alone a pirate, this way when my lover was putting everything on the line to be with me? Madame Chevalier may have been a hundred miles away and I might never get back to her but she was mine and I was hers. I was her pearl. She was waiting for me, and there I was climaxing to the sight of another woman. By the time I had trodden down the stairs to Petra, I had decided that I deserved whatever heap of misery the day would bring, and I would take it without complaint.

Chapter Eleven

As I settled into my working routine over the next few days, the captain never spoke of what I had seen that night or what she knew I had been doing under that blanket. Every time the memory surfaced it caused a rush of embarrassment to flood through me but also brought such an ache to my core it was overwhelming. However much I told myself I did not want her, I could not stop myself looking at Captain Halliwell and wondering what those full lips of hers would feel like on mine. I told myself that it was just because I saw her every day and she was the only nice thing on this ship to look at that I could not stem the rush of heat in my veins. She never did anything by halves. She was either a raging fire or impenetrable stone and the promise of excitement and danger stirred something within me. She fascinated me. She terrified me. She occupied my mind in a way that no one else had.

I had been thinking about her after a long day and I had just curled up in my corner to await the sweet bliss of unconsciousness that was my only reprieve from the hard labor of sea life when the captain stormed into the cabin.

"Filthy cheating lowlifes," she growled as she slammed the door shut hard enough to make me jump.

The motion attracted her attention, and she turned her furious gaze on me. Instinctively I scrambled away from her until my back hit the wall. She froze and a pained expression flitted across her features. Before I could say a word, she had turned and stomped over to a small round table in the corner that had sat unused for my entire time aboard the Bone Heart and dragged it out along with two chairs that had been tucked under it.

"Come here, sweetpea."

I kept my wary gaze on her as I dropped my blanket and stood.

"For goodness sake, you are not in trouble. Come here," the captain said exasperatedly and gestured for me to sit at the table with her. She slung her coat over the back of her chair. "Do you know how to play cards?"

"Of course not, it's a game for…" I slammed my mouth closed before I could repeat my mother's words on card games being for ruffians and uncouth men.

The captain's mouth quirked as if she knew exactly what I had been about to say. Her fingers moved deftly as she shuffled the deck.

"You want me to play cards with you?" I asked, frowning in confusion.

"Is that a problem?" she asked, a steely glint in her eye as if daring me to refuse.

"Not at all. I just… why me? And not one of the crew."

"Dishonest cheats the lot of them," Captain Halliwell scoffed, but her tone had lost all of its earlier fury so that she said it almost fondly. "I've almost forgotten what it's like to play an honest opponent."

She dealt the worn and stained playing cards facedown between us and at her nod, I picked up my pile.

"I'll walk you through a round and then we play," the captain said, adjusting her own cards in her hand and then showing them to me. "What do you have?"

I stared at the unfamiliar symbols for a moment, dumbfounded.

"You really have never played, have you? What a good girl following the rules."

Before I could utter a retort, she rounded the table

with a wicked smirk.

The captain strode behind me and leant forward to look at my cards. She was so close that if I turned my head, I could have buried my face in the crook of her neck and breathed her in. Warmth crept across my cheeks. She did not need to be this close to me. I could have shown her my cards from across the table. I bit my lip. I could feel the smirk in her tone as she explained what the different cards were. She knew she was making me squirm and was doing it on purpose for her own amusement and I hated that I did not hate it.

I could hardly focus with her mouth so close to my ear as she explained the rules of the game in a low murmur. She must have been shouting at the crew a lot today because her voice had a slightly hoarse rasp to it as she spoke.

"Got it?"

"Yes," I lied.

"Good."

I flinched as she squeezed my shoulder.

"Don't look so scared sweetpea. It's only a game," she grinned as she returned to her seat.

"I have nothing to wager," I blurted.

"Do you not?"

I frowned at her. Where on earth did she think I was hiding any valuables? I had nothing. Less than nothing and she knew that. I went from living in a manor with anything I wished for at my beck and call and now I barely had claim to a patch of cold, hard floor in Captain Halliwell's cabin.

"You know I have nothing but the clothes on my back," I huffed in bitterness without thinking.

The look that the captain gave me sent an explosion of shivers down my spine. My irritation was forgotten in a second as her dark eyes trailed down my body as she cocked her head to the side.

"What an interesting proposal."

"What?" I squeaked. "No! I did not mean—"

Captain Halliwell cut off my protests with a loud guffaw.

"You are just too precious, sweetpea. You need to learn to relax." As if to demonstrate, she leaned back in her chair, rolled her sleeves to her elbows and stretched, cat-like and still grinning. "We'll forgo the usual wagers. Don't worry your pretty head about it."

A small "alright" was all I could manage in response. I would be lying if I said I could focus on my cards at that moment in time and gave myself a vigorous mental shake.

My fingertips traced marks on the table as I tried to calm myself and banish the idea of betting items of clothing with the captain from my mind. The surface was marred with dents and holes that looked like someone had stabbed a knife into it.

"It's from five finger filet." The captain answered my unasked question. "And no, sweetpea, I will not be teaching you that game. As amusing as it would be to watch you slice your fingers to bits trying to be a big bad pirate, I still don't want you damaged. Not yet anyway."

She winked at me and threw a card down in the center of the table.

When I looked at her blankly, she rolled her eyes and guided me through the first few moves with the air of someone talking to a child. The more patronizing she became, the more motivated I was to win and make her eat her words. It would be glorious to knock the infuriating woman down a peg or two. I grit my teeth and tried to focus.

We did not speak as we played, and Captain Halliwell shot down any attempt I made at small talk, but I found that I actually enjoyed playing once the game got going even though she saw through every move I made.

The captain had no qualms about completely destroying me at our first game even though I had barely a grasp of the rules. The second and third passed similarly and my frustration was mounting but so was my fatigue. I stifled a yawn with the back of my hand as she threw down yet another set of winning cards with a smug grin.

"I would not have thought winning against me would bring you such joy. I am hardly a worthy opponent," I grumbled, tossing my own cards next to hers.

"Oh, sweetpea, winning always brings me joy."

My retort was lost in another yawn.

"One more hand, sweetpea," Captain Halliwell said as she gathered up the cards again and smirked as I groaned. "I'm not done with you just yet."

Chapter Twelve

Captain Halliwell still claimed it was purely due to boredom and the fact that the rest of the crew were likely to cheat, but we played cards almost every night. I never did manage to win but I at least learned enough to make it a challenge for her. We did not speak much during those hours as was her preference, but it was a comfortable silence and whatever she chose to tell herself, I knew she enjoyed my company. She certainly seemed to enjoy staring at me when she thought I was focused on my cards. It made something low in my belly spark every time I noticed it.

Even with the inconvenience of my attraction to her, as the days went by, we were becoming something more like friends and less like captain and stowaway. I saw less of her anger that she used as a shield and more of the woman underneath. I saw her smile and laugh and, on the rare occasions that we did speak, a glint would appear in her eyes as she spoke of faraway places and the thrill of adventure. Any attempt to coax stories from her, however, were met with a snort and a bark to play my next card.

I was undeterred, however, and each night I tried to unravel more of her mystery until she inevitably, wearily, told me to hush or threatened to sew my lips shut. But every night, she asked me to play again.

Of course, my days were still filled with back-breaking labor, and I worked until I ached in the kitchens or anywhere else that needed cleaning. Fortunately, I was never tasked with the goat's care again, but I did occasionally have to gut fish that the crew caught which was almost as nauseating.

I was sweeping the galley –a task I had decided was one of the more preferable ones –when Captain Halliwell barreled into the kitchen with such an air of urgency that even Petra froze halfway through chopping a fish head off with a cleaver.

We had been at sea for almost two weeks without incident. Now however, it appeared we were closing in on our destination—a destination that the captain had neglected to tell me no matter how many times I asked where we were going.

"We're coming up on Siren's Cove," Captain Halliwell said, holding something out to me. "Put these in your ears and go to the cabin. Petra, storm's coming."

I raised my eyebrows in derision at the blobs of wax she had given me. "You are superstitious, captain?"

The look she gave me reminded me that although it felt that she was warming towards me, sometimes teetering on the verge of genuine affection, there was still a part of her that was just as likely to toss me overboard as she had ever been if I questioned her.

"Mind your tongue," she snapped. "Put those in now and do not take them out until I tell you otherwise. Why are you still here? I told you to go to the cabin."

I was not going to turn down an opportunity to stop working early. I dropped the broom and made my escape before she could change her mind.

"Put that wax in!" she yelled at me as I hurried up the stairs.

The captain had not lied when she said a storm was coming. As I surfaced from the kitchens onto the deck, the skies were blackening and the clouds rolling with a horrible growling. The wind and rain had not yet started but the air was heavy, and I could taste it on my tongue. I raced the last few steps to the captain's cabin just as fat, wet drops started to fall.

In minutes, the ship was rocking more than it ever had, and it sent my stomach lurching. I had never been troubled by seasickness, but then again, I had never been aboard a ship that was truly at the mercy of the elements.

Before long, rain was lashing at the windows, and I could hear the ship groaning from all sides. Thunder so loud that it shook the floorboards roared directly overhead and cracks of lightning illuminated the dark cabin. I had not lit any lanterns in case they upended and set the cabin alight. I sat in the dark, alone and terrified. I even risked the captain's wrath by huddling up in her chair rather than my corner.

I still had the balls of wax clenched in my hand. There was no way I was going to deafen myself and not give myself warning when the ceiling came in or the mast crashed through the deck. Not only that, but what if I was unable to get the wax out again? Would I be deafened forever? I thought of all the beautiful music I had enjoyed over the years. The more I thought about it, the more I could practically hear the violins over the howling wind. I would not risk losing that. Not over the captain's silly superstitions. Another crack of lightning had me flinching and hugging my knees to my chest just like I had as a child when the summer storms had rolled into shore.

I frowned. I was a child no longer and I really needed to pull myself together. I was a grown woman. I had stowed away on a ship, heading for a life of love and adventure for goodness' sake. I gave myself a shake. It was just a little bad weather.

I had always been a little anxious in the dark, though, ever since I was a small child. Not being able to see always made me nervous. Well, I smiled to myself at the sudden memory, almost always.

Madame's Studio

"My dearest pearl, I feel like you are not even trying today," Madame scolded lightly as she reviewed my progress.

She was utterly correct. I had no interest in painting the bowl of fruit that sat in front of me. I had, in fact, not wanted to paint at all today and had hoped that we could simply pursue more interesting activities for the afternoon. Madame had just returned from a trip to a nearby town and I had not seen her in over a week.

"Tell me the mistakes you have made," she said, resting her hands on my shoulders from where she stood behind me.

I sighed and leaned back so that my head rested on her stomach. "Must we do this now? Have you not missed me?"

"Of course, my pearl. But your education comes first, does it not?"

I smiled sweetly up at her. "Perhaps you could educate me in other matters?"

"Pay attention." She tutted and tilted my head so that I looked at my lackluster painting instead of at her. "What have you done wrong?"

"I do not know," I huffed. "Tell me so that I may correct it."

"My impatient girl," Madame said fondly, stroking my hair. "Look at the bowl."

"I am looking."

"Then why is your painting wrong?"

I bit my lip at her tone. Madame may have taken me as a lover, but that did not mean she accepted any failings from me as her student and had hinted more than once that others might be more deserving of her tutelage. I could not bear to disappoint her.

"My apologies, Madame. I truly do not know."

She circled around so that she was facing me and

cupped my cheeks.

"You are looking but you are not seeing." At my confused frown, she continued, "You are painting what you think you see and not what you truly see."

"I do not think I understand."

"Hm." She tilted her head and gave me a secretive smile. "Perhaps you simply need a break. A little distraction, hm?"

Her laugh was a tinkling of bells as I perked up immediately. She entwined her fingers with mine and led me away from my failed painting.

"Shall we try something new?" she whispered as we crossed the threshold into her bedroom.

I shivered in delight at the lust coating her words. Everything with her had been new to me. From my first kiss to the first time she took me to her bedroom. She introduced me to height of feelings I had thought only existed in books.

"Always," I whispered back as she directed me to stand by the bed.

"Close your eyes."

I did so immediately. Her hand left mine to trail up my arm and along my shoulders, grazing up the side of my neck and along my jaw. I opened my eyes and playfully snapped my teeth at her fingertips.

"Now, now. None of that," she admonished, tapping me lightly on the tip of my nose. "Close your eyes, pearl. Good things come to those who wait."

Her hands left me and I stood, trying not to fidget, as I heard her retrieve something from a drawer.

I gasped as soft fabric covered my eyes.

"Since your difficulty today seems to be with seeing what is in front of you, I thought we would remove that particular challenge," she whispered as she tied the silken blindfold snugly around my head. "Now, be still."

My belly coiled in excitement and apprehension as

she undressed me. She took her time, but soon the last of my clothing fell away. I shivered, my nipples pebbling with exposure and desire. Cool hands on my hips. A hot mouth on my neck. I moaned and pressed my thighs together, aching for her touch.

All too soon, her touch left me.

"Madame Chevalier?" I whispered.

She did not respond. I itched to tear away my blindfold but that would ruin her game. I had already disappointed her once that day so now I would do whatever she asked of me. I could hear her, though, as she moved away from me followed by the soft plink as she dropped each of her rings, one by one, into the dish she kept on her side table. Then I could not hear her at all.

I could feel every breath of air against my skin and my own pulse hammering in my ears. The carpet was soft as I dug my toes into it, trying my best to stay still for her. I knew instantly when she had returned to my side, and I breathed a sigh of relief. She had not left me.

Again, she did not say a word but her hands on my body guided me to the bed. I climbed up but, instead of laying me down like I expected, Madame guided me to my knees in the center of the mattress. She climbed up with me. From the way fabric slid against my bare skin, I knew she had not disrobed at all. I swiveled my head to where I thought her face must be.

"Relax, my pearl. I am here."

I swallowed and nodded as her fingers kneaded my shoulders. I leaned into her massage. It was pleasant and intimate but not what I really wanted.

"Patience," she whispered, as if sensing my thoughts.

I groaned as she lightly dragged her manicured nails down my back. I arched my spine.

"I want to touch you," I whispered and then flinched in surprise when her hand came around to cover my mouth.

The back of my head was pressed against her ample chest as her free hand came to my own breast.

Without my sight, every touch became amplified and, as she rolled my nipple between her finger and thumb, the sensation shot straight between my legs. My moans of pleasure were muffled by her palm as she gave my other nipple the same attention before kneading the soft flesh. Teeth grazed my earlobe, then my jaw. I was soon squirming as she nibbled and sucked all the way down to my collarbone. Her ministrations were not anything she had not done to me before, but I felt them all so much more clearly. When her hand left my mouth so that she could tend to both my breasts at once, I felt I might explode. As one hand ventured down my belly and between my legs, I knew it was going to take no time at all until I really did explode.

My legs shook and my hands fisted in the sheets beneath me as Madame coaxed me towards release with her fingers.

I was close. So close. So close. So—

Her touch left me and I bucked into thin air. Confusion, frustration, even a tinge of anger coursed through me as I came down from the heights she had brought me to. Why did she do that?

"No!" was all I could gasp.

Her hands were back at my nipples, firing them up once more.

"Why did you stop?" I whined, hating how desperate I sounded.

"Oh, now I have your full attention?"

"You always have my attention," I panted, tipping my head back against her.

"It seemed to me that you have stopped appreciating my lessons."

"Never…Madame Chevalier, please…"

She was back between my legs, and I moaned as she

sunk two fingers into me.

"Will you try harder?" She withdrew and pushed back in, torturously slow.

"Yes!" I cried out as she curled her fingers inside me.

"Will you stop making such silly mistakes?" Again the same cruel teasing.

"Yes!"

"Are you sorry?" This time she drove them in with more force and I jerked against her, desperate for more.

"Yes!"

She withdrew her fingers from me, removed the blindfold from my eyes and leaned back against the headboard, lifting her skirts. She wore nothing underneath.

"Come and show me how sorry you are, my pearl."

I believe I had truly done my best work that evening, and none of it with a paintbrush. I had asked her afterwards if maybe I could blindfold her sometime and tease her like she had done to me. Oh, what I would have given to have that stern woman writhe under my touch and plead for release. She was always in control and seeing her lose it would have been a delight. The thought of it, even now, sent a jolt of heat through me. Sadly, she had declined saying I was far too pleasing to the eye for her to not look at.

Thinking of Madame brought with it a heaviness I not anticipated, and it was enough to make me let out a sigh. She had not crossed my mind in days and the thought of being her pearl once more did not bring the rush of joy and hope that had kept me going when I first found myself aboard the Bone Heart. I was more uncertain than ever what the future held for me. I now did not dream of island paradise with my once painting tutor nor did I dream of Beauris high society life. I did not truly fit anywhere anymore.

Reminiscing on that night we spent together had, however, done a good job in distracting me from the storm. It even seemed to be letting up. I had thought the raging sea would have continued its tirade for hours, but it seemed that it was not ready to claim the Bone Heart quite yet. The howling winds had settled to a stiff breeze, and the windows were no longer being assaulted by the downpour. I stood from where I had been curled in my childish fear and stretched out my legs. My muscles ached fiercely despite the relatively light work load of the day.

"Sweetpea!"

The captain's yell cut through the last dregs of the storm, but she did not sound angry.

"Sweetpea, come here!"

I edged out of the cabin, reluctantly. The captain's summons were usually followed by unpleasant tasks, but I could hardly ignore them however much I wished to.

The lashing rain had calmed to a drizzle as I opened the door and peeked out. I would still get wet if I ventured outside so I hesitated at the door.

Thunder rolled again but as a distant echo.

"Sweetpea!" The call came again, and I squinted to find the captain on deck. The rest of the crew must be below, sheltering from the storm, I thought. There was no delaying it any longer. I ducked out into the rain. Fat drops ran down the back of my neck, plastering my hair to my skin but it was pleasantly warm. We must have travelled farther south than I had realized.

The captain was soaked too. Raindrops glittered as they ran down her face that she had turned up to the sky.

"Look," she said as I reached her. She took my shoulders with uncharacteristic gentleness and turned me so that I was looking out across the now calm sea.

A rainbow stretched as far as the eye could see. My mouth dropped open. I had never seen such clear color before. It looked like someone had taken a paintbrush to the sky.

The captain squeezed my shoulders. "I thought you

would like it, Elise."

I frowned. "You have never called me Elise before."

A dolphin leapt from the waves, chattering playfully.

"Why wouldn't I? It's such a lovely name." Her voice was buttery soft in my ear.

She had never spoken to me so softly either. I tried to turn to look at her, but she wrapped her arms around me.

"Are you ill? What is wrong with you?"

Her soft laugh rumbled against my back. "Nothing is wrong. Doesn't this feel right?"

I shook my head. "This…this is not right."

"Just look at the rainbow, Elise. Isn't it beautiful?"

I wriggled out of her embrace.

I whirled, intending to demand what her game was and tell her I was not interested in being the punchline of whatever joke she was surely playing on me, only the words died in my mouth.

"Cap…captain?"

Her dark eyes were now fully black with no trace of white around the edges. Oh lord.

"Just look at the rainbow, Elise." Her smile had too many teeth.

"What are you!?"

I staggered and my back hit the railing. When did I move closer to the railing? Whatever wore the captain's face matched my steps. A hand with nails that were too sharp reached for me. I screamed and ducked around the outstretched arm.

I ran a few paces before realizing there was nowhere to go. The thing smiled and took a step towards me. It had started raining again and my vision blurred.

"What's wrong, Elise? I thought you liked me?"

"You are not her!" I yelled back.

I glanced around desperately for an escape. On the other side of the ship, I caught a flash of green and white amongst the blue. Land! I could swim to safety!

"No!" The monster with the captain's face cried as they saw what I had seen, their voice deepening so much that I felt it rattle in my chest. "What are you doing?"

"Getting away from you!" I screamed as I launched myself towards the opposite railing. "I will not be eaten! I will not!"

I had one leg up on railing and was about to launch myself into the now churning sea below when something wrapped around me from behind and pulled me back. I lost my grip and cried out, fighting against whatever held me. A horrid gray arm was wrapped firmly around my middle, and I could not shift it. I shrieked and fought as I was dragged along the deck. I had to get to the railing. I had to get off the ship. Rain pelted from the sky, blinding me.

The creature pulled me close to its chest, entrapping me. In a last desperate attempt to free myself, I stopped resisting and instead threw my weight towards the monster that had dared to wear the captain's image. Surprise registered on its distorted features as I bowled it over and raked my nails down its face. Its scream was the most horrible sound I had ever heard. Like shattering glass inside my skull.

I pulled myself free from the appendages and once more tried for the railing. My knees hit the deck hard. For a moment, I thought I had slipped on the wet planks before the clawed hand wrapped around my ankle started to pull. The deck slipped under my fingertips as I scrabbled for purchase that was nowhere to be found.

My blood froze in my veins as it reared up to its full height before me, sword in hand. The last thing I saw was the distorted, monstrous face of the captain, twisted in rage as she brought it down on my head.

Chapter Thirteen

I floated in and out of consciousness like driftwood on the tide until it was brutally tossed upon the rocks. I groaned as I awoke fully. Everything hurt. Had I taken ill?

I squinted. This was not my bedroom. The ground lurched.

"Oh," I groaned again as my misadventure came back to me.

Of course, I was in Captain Halliwell's cabin. I frowned. I had never seen it from this angle. I was on the wrong side of the room. Oh lord. I was in the captain's bunk. She was going to be furious with me. However I had gotten there, I needed to get out before she murdered me.

The blanket was wrapped around me like a stifling cocoon and sweat had begun beading on my forehead. For several long minutes, I thought I was truly stuck until something shifted and I could work one arm free.

I tried to sit up to unravel myself, but a wave of nausea had me sinking back into the pillow, moaning. I lifted my free hand to my aching head. My fingertips met fabric, and a jolt of pain shot through my head at the touch. I stiffened in alarm. I was injured? Was I bleeding? What happened? Blinking did nothing to help my blurred vision, and gentle probing informed me that one of my eyes was swollen and tender. I felt like I had been tossed around on the open seas instead of merely being aboard a ship that had been.

The storm. I remembered the storm.

"Lord, what happened?" I mumbled.

"You are a damned fool, that's what happened."

I instinctively swiveled to look and regretted it as the motion sent my insides lurching and bile threatened to claw its way up my throat.

"Captain." I squeezed my eyes shut. "I…I do not know why I am in your bed—"

"Because I put you there. Here."

The captain's hand supported the back of my neck as a cup was held to my lips. The water was cool in my mouth, and I savored the small sip I was given. Water was a precious resource, after all. Petra had informed me many times that it was wasted on me.

I sighed and let my head fall back. The sheets in the bunk were rough and smelled slightly musty. My eyes snapped open. I could feel exactly how rough the sheets were. I was completely naked underneath them.

"Why am I undressed?" I gasped. "Why—Oh lord."

The captain had come around to sit beside the bunk on the low, three-legged stool that was usually mine. Her hair hung in damp locks about her face, and shadows of exhaustion made bags under her eyes. But that was not what made the breath catch in my throat. Three vicious scratches ran from just below her left eye all the way down her cheek.

Oh.

I glanced at my fingernails and then back at her face in dismay.

"Captain, I am so sorry. I thought you were a monster." I frowned, my head pulsing. "Why did I think that? What is wrong with me?"

"You are a fool who doesn't do as she is told," the captain snarled but it lacked strength. Her voice softened as her eyes scanned my face. "I told you to block your ears and stay in the cabin."

I huffed out a laugh.

"You cannot tell me that sirens got into my head."

Her expression was grave.

"You've been asleep for two days after trying to throw yourself overboard. How else do you explain it?"

"Two days?" I squeaked. "Oh lord I must have caught the fever or something."

"Fever." Captain Halliwell snorted. "Call it what you want, sweetpea. Have you ever heard of a fever making someone want to take a nice swim?"

I wriggled in my sheets and ignored her question. Sirens were not real and I refused to entertain her superstitions. "I am overheating. Help me out of this."

"You're staying wrapped up warm," she said firmly, resting a hand on my shoulder to stop me from rising. "Besides, I would prefer you not to be able to move much until I am certain there's no more siren devilry in your mind and you take another swing at me. Not that you did me much damage, but you were lost to it and trying to throw yourself overboard. I had to incapacitate you."

I groaned.

"Incapacitate…What on earth did you hit me with? I feel like I took a cannon ball to the head."

She did not answer but instead reached out to grip my chin, tilting my face to the side to squint into my eyes.

"I assure you, I am quite myself, captain," I said, shaking her off.

I attempted, again, to extricate myself from my fabric prison and then slumped as a fresh wave of pain rattled around my skull.

"You'll make it worse if you don't settle down."

She took hold of the back of my neck and again a cup was brought to my lips. Instead of water, a fiery spirit coated my tongue and I coughed. The captain did not let up, though, and made me drink half a cupful. I did not fail to notice that her touch lingered after she had set the cup aside, nor the raw concern in her dark eyes.

"Nothing better to warm the soul after a brush with the spirits."

That did not sound like something the captain would say. She caught my suspicious look and added, "Something my nana used to say."

"Tell me about her."

I closed my eyes and settled back into the bunk. It was wonderful to lay on something soft for once. Whatever was in the drink she had given me was pleasantly swirling in my belly.

"Shh. Another time, sweetpea. Rest, that's an order." The captain stroked my hair and lowered her voice. "The crew is under the impression that you are not only recovering from the sirens but from the sound beating you received for not following orders. Am I clear?"

I swallowed thickly. "You are not going to deliver that beating, are you?"

"No, sweetpea," she murmured, still stroking my hair. "You have suffered enough in my eyes, but the crew would not see it that way. If pressed, you are to say that you were suitably punished for your disobedience, understand?"

"I understand," I whispered. "Thank you, captain."

"You may stay in the bunk for now."

"Where will you sleep?" My tongue was heavy and the words slid over each other.

"My chair will suffice. I shall only grab a few hours, anyway. The storm was fierce. The Heart is a tough old girl, but we've still got repairs to do before we can think of going anywhere."

"Thank you," I murmured again.

"Don't get used to it," she sighed tipping her hat down low over her eyes as she settled down into her chair. "One night, maybe two, until you're feeling better then you're back on the floor where you belong."

Chapter Fourteen

Sometime as I slumbered fitfully, the captain must have had a change of heart about letting me rest because I awoke to Sully hammering nails into the wall of the cabin, his floppy hair flying with each blow.

"What on earth are you doing?!" I cried, clutching my head.

"Oh, sorry."

As he turned to look at me, his face flushed bright red all the way to the tips of his ears. I had forgotten I still was not wearing a scrap of clothing and tugged the sheets closer around my body. He had hardly seen any more than the rest of the crew already had, but I still felt my own face heat.

He cleared his throat and his gaze flickered to the bandages around my head and my general sorry state.

"Are you...well?" he asked nervously. "There's some whispers flying that the sirens got to you."

I huffed out a chuckle and propped myself up. "I do not imagine there are such things as sirens. But I am quite well. Or I will be soon. Thank you for your concern."

I blinked at the bright sunlight streaming in through the windows. The ship was hardly even rocking.

"Have we made port?" I sat up straighter. If we had made land, then perhaps I would have the chance to flee. Where I would flee to, how I would survive alone or even where in the world I was, I had no idea. The idea melted from my mind as quickly as it had appeared and I slumped in the bunk a little.

Sully shook his head. "Nay, but we've dropped anchor. We're making repairs and then we'll make the dive soon."

"Dive? What dive? To a shipwreck? Treasure?" My mind was suddenly alight with all of the stories of sunken ships and adventure I had read as a child.

Sully frowned. "I suppose if the cap'n hasn't told you, then I shouldn't say."

I tried to coax more out of the boy, but he refused and lifted his hammer to the wall again. I braced myself for the impending headache.

"You have still neglected to tell me what you are doing in here or is that another secret that I am not privy to?" I asked, petulantly.

"Oh, I thought that was obvious." He gestured to a bundle of canvas at his feet. "Captain said she wanted a hammock put up for you. Guess she is sweet on you, after all."

"Excuse me?" Laughter burst from my lips. "The captain is absolutely not sweet on me."

I remembered the captain's words and quickly added, "I was punished for disobeying her orders."

"Whatever you say." He grinned at me. "But we all saw her when she thought you were going overboard."

That gave me pause. She had been scared for me. She saved my life. Brutish, arrogant and coarse as she may be, there was no denying that the captain had come to care for me in her own way.

I tried to question Sully more on what had actually happened, but he was tightlipped.

As soon as the boy left, I jumped up to inspect my new hammock. After hanging onto the desk for a few minutes until my head stopped spinning, I felt stable enough to walk the few steps to the other side of the cabin, taking the sheets from the bunk with me.

The hammock was a gift. There was nothing else to

call it. I let myself smile. Sully was right. I had often suspected that she cared for me more than she liked to admit, and this just proved it.

"If you annoy me, I shall take it back."

I whipped around to see Captain Halliwell standing in the doorway. She had shed her customary red coat and her hat, and her sleeves were rolled to her elbows. Her hair hung damp around her face like she had been caught in the rain once again, but her eyes sparkled with humor.

"Good to see you're up and about, sweetpea." She actually smiled.

"Thank you," I stammered. "For the hammock, I mean."

A pink tinge appeared on the captain's cheeks as she shrugged. "You need rest to heal properly if I'm to get paid, and I'm not giving up my bunk any longer for a measly stowaway."

"Ah, I see. This is all so that you get your coin at the end of the day and not at all because you have grown to care for me." I arched an eyebrow.

She snorted. "Of course not."

I touched the side of the hammock and tested some of my weight on it. It did not feel very stable. I had not the slightest idea how I was supposed to get into it.

"How does one…?"

I squeaked as the captain scooped me up in her arms and laid me down in the nest of fabric.

"There." She grinned at my shocked expression, but shock was not the only thing that stole my ability to speak in that moment.

I had known the captain was strong, but I had never expected her to lift me so effortlessly. Being held in her muscular arms, even for a moment, was almost enough to make me swoon. The way my body was pressed against hers… I cleared my throat, trying to recover, but by the twinkle in her eye and the curl of her smirk, the captain knew very well what effect she had just had on me.

"How—" I had to clear my throat again and it only made her infuriating smile grow wider. "How do I get out again?"

"I imagine you'll fall out."

"That is not funny."

"Agree to disagree. I'm needed on deck, but I'll see to it that Petra brings you some soup. Sleep tight, sweetpea."

Chapter Fifteen

I did indeed fall out of my new hammock. Multiple times. But, to my pride, I managed to get back in without assistance.

For a few days, Petra brought me food, unbandaged my head and scolded me relentlessly for not blocking my ears as I was told to in the first place despite my protests that sirens had nothing to do with my illness. I seldom saw Captain Halliwell and, when I did, it was only when she came in late at night and she fell asleep immediately and left again early. The ship stayed anchored the whole time. Whatever they were diving for, it was taking time. I wondered if they could not find what they were looking for or had found it but simply lacked the means retrieve it.

I had very much enjoyed my few days of relaxation. My poor muscles were finally recovering from life at sea, but I was beginning to get restless. I wanted to know what was going on. I was surprised to find that I wanted to be a part of it. I might not have been part of the crew but, right now, it was all I had. Decision made, I flopped out of my hammock, washed, dressed and made my way on deck.

I was not prepared for the sight that met me. *Gold.*

It flowed out of what looked like a huge, ceramic jug. The cracked sides were covered in paintings of strange creatures and patterns that I had never seen before. A relic of some forgotten civilization. The crew whooped as it thundered onto the deck. Ceramic shards littered the planks, indicating that this was not the first haul.

"Get that gathered up now!" the captain barked. "If even one coin rolls overboard, I'm sending you in to get it! And if I find them in any man's pockets, I'll hang him from the main sail!"

Her words were harsh but her tone jovial and a true smile stretched across her face. Gold was the one thing that could ensure morale on board, and I knew she had been worried about the mood of the crew for a while even if she did not say the words.

The men snapped into action and started stuffing it into large canvas sacks while hollering about what they would spend their share on. The general consensus was women and rum.

"Your attention, gents!" The captain hopped up onto the railing to a chorus of cheers. "I know some of you doubted this venture, but I hope your doubts have been satisfied now that I've made us richer than a king's galleon!"

The roar that sprung up at her words was deafening.

"I've quenched your doubts and filled your purses! So tonight, let's quench our thirst and fill our bellies! Petra! Bring out the rum!"

The longer we had been at sea, the more the standard of the food declined as we ran out of fresh produce and started on the salted meats, pickled vegetables and hard biscuits. Tonight though, seasoned with victory, it tasted magnificent. Everyone ate together sitting under the cool night sky, and bottles of rum were passed around while the pirates belted out their favorite sea shanties.

I kept to the sidelines, watching the merriment and nibbling on a biscuit. I was sure that if they remembered I was there, I would be shooed away. This was a night of celebration for the crew, and I was not a part of that crew.

However, my presence did not go unnoticed for long as Captain Halliwell sidled over to where I was lounging against a barrel.

"I believe congratulations are in order," I said.

"Aye. We'll be as rich as royalty." She took a deep breath, seeming to savor the statement.

"Good to see you're feeling better," the captain added, her eyes grazing over my face and up to where the bump on my head was hidden by my hair.

"I am." I cleared my throat. "And thank you again for the hammock. It is much more comfortable."

The captain grinned as she leaned over and plucked the biscuit from my fingers. "After this haul, everyone will be getting an upgrade when we next make port."

She popped the last of my biscuit into her mouth and chuckled as I pouted.

"I've had enough of these hooligans for one night. I've got something better for us in the cabin." She winked. "Come with me."

Captain Halliwell led me back to her cabin and pulled out the small round table that we used for cards. We had not played in some days and I perked up at the thought of a game. She gestured to one of the chairs but instead of reaching for the deck, she stooped to unlock one of the drawers of her desk.

"I've been saving this for a special occasion," she said as she straightened up holding a bottle. "Those scoundrels out there wouldn't appreciate a wine such as this, but I imagine you have a taste for the finer things."

"You are sharing it with me?"

She shrugged. "One should not drink alone."

The wine was a deep red as the captain poured two glasses. She swirled it and inhaled deeply, cherishing the scent, before taking a sip. A smile spread across her face. Even as tired as she was looking these days, she was still beautiful when she smiled.

I sipped my own wine before she could catch me staring. It was rich and heavy on my tongue.

"Wonderful!" I exclaimed, and she grinned back at

me.

"As it should be. I got this from my first sea battle as captain. The navy officer who captained the other ship had fine taste in wine."

She leaned back in her chair with a grin and propped her boots up on the table.

I shuddered at the mention of battle. Every time I forgot just how bloodthirsty these pirates probably were, they found some opportunity to remind me. That other captain likely did not survive the fight.

I set my glass down.

"Were you always a pirate?"

Captain Halliwell cocked her head, and I could tell she was deciding whether she was going to answer me truthfully or with a jest.

"No," she decided finally. "I found myself a pirate due to unfortunate circumstances."

"What circumstances?"

"Unfortunate ones." She winked at me over the rim of her glass.

"Tell me how you became captain, then," I replied, rolling my eyes.

"I told you. I had a tutor."

At my pout, she sighed.

"The late captain of this ship was my mentor. I took over when he died."

"What happened to him?"

"You ask a lot of questions."

"I am hardly blessed with many opportunities to converse with pirates, and you are not always so forthcoming with answers. Indulge me, captain."

Captain Halliwell took a slow sip of her wine before she answered.

"I, not unlike yourself, took a questionable lover. I was young and didn't know what I was getting myself into.

Her husband found out."

I covered my mouth with my hands to hide my gasp.

The captain gave a grim nod. "He followed me one night when I left the inn where we used to meet in secret. I never saw it coming. He snuck up on me. The next thing I knew, there was a knife in my gut, and I was taking a swan dive into the harbor."

She removed her boots from the table and lifted her shirt to show me a small scar just under her ribs.

"I would have drowned had the previous captain of this ship not been drinking on the dock and witnessed the whole thing. Took it as an offering from God to redeem his soul if he saved me. So, he did. Brought me on board and trained me up." She took another long drink. "He was a good captain. He should have stayed captain for another ten years at least. I thought I would have more time."

How many others had she shared this story with? I could not imagine it being many if it were a story where she had needed to be saved. Who would she have been if not for that night? Someone softer, maybe? I knew there was gentleness in her even if she hid it from the world. I wanted to reach out and trace the scar with my fingertips. Perhaps I might have if there had not been a table between us.

"What happened to him? The previous captain?" I asked as she tucked her shirt back into her trousers.

"Damn bad luck, that's what happened," she replied bitterly. "He got sick, and we were far out at sea and couldn't get him medicine in time. He deserved a better death than that."

"I'm sorry," I murmured.

"After that, it was a choice between the old first mate and myself. We fought it out and I won. I don't think some of the crew have gotten over that. Old Lucky was well liked."

"Have you…" I shuddered. "Have you killed many people?"

"A fair few." She cocked her head to the side, and in a low voice asked, "Does that scare you?"

"Yes," I admitted. "You scare me quite a bit."

Although not for the reasons you may think. I left that part unsaid.

Of course, her violence scared me but what truly terrified me the most was how much I wanted her anyway. I wanted her fire and passion. I wanted that incredible body, that sharp mind and that hidden soul that I let myself believe that she showed only to me.

"But I doubt that you are truly a bad person at heart," I said.

She laughed. "I'm too soft on you if you think that."

I gave an unladylike snort. "You are not soft on me at all. Although you are not as cruel as I feared you might be after that first day."

The regret that flitted across her features was painfully clear.

"I know you had to do it," I murmured.

I do not know what possessed me to reach across the table and take her hand, but I was surprised and pleased when she let me. Her palm was rough but warm and I let my thumb trace over her knuckles. The map of tiny scars across her skin told of many stories filled with violence. I wanted to hear them all. I wanted to know her.

She cleared her throat and shook her head as if the intimacy had suddenly made her uncomfortable. I sighed as I saw the walls she had built around her heart slide firmly back into place.

"What's done is done," she said flatly, taking her hand back to pour us both another glass.

She smirked as she topped up my wine. "Tell me more about your secret lover."

I cringed. The unfaithfulness of my desire was the last thing I wished to be reminded of. "What do you want to know?"

Captain Halliwell shrugged. "What was she like?"

She is…" I struggled over the words. The captain said 'was'…past tense. Were Madame and I in truly the past? It seemed foolish now to imagine that I would find her again. The Bone Heart would be delivering me home to Beauris, not to Mulla where she was waiting for me. If she was still waiting for me, that was. It was long past the time we were supposed to meet. If I were in her position, I would assume I had been lost to the sea. If the choice were mine, would I want to find her again? That dark question had been visiting me late at night lately and robbing me of my sleep. I was not the same young woman who had left Beauris. Would Madame still want me? Did I still want her?

I took a sip of wine to cover my dilemma. It was difficult to even summon the image of Madame when this beautiful dangerous woman was staring deep into my eyes.

"Tall," I said eventually.

"Tall," Captain Halliwell repeated, raising an eyebrow in amusement. "Is that all?"

"No!" I retorted with a huff, setting my glass down with more force than was necessary. "She is highly intelligent. Elegant. She cares for me, even if she is a little stern sometimes, I'll admit."

"Stern, hm?" Captain Halliwell's smile turned wicked. "So, you like being ordered around? I shall keep that in mind."

"I did not say that!" I flustered but her grin simply grew, no doubt because my cheeks had reddened. In all of our time together, mercilessly teasing me seemed to still be her favorite past time.

"So, what do you like, sweetpea?" Her voice lowered into a purr. A suggestive purr that left no doubt in my mind that the question was not an innocent one. Heat flickered in my core. I swallowed hard. I should not indulge this, I told myself.

"That is private." I had tried to sound stern, to shut the conversation down before it went too far, but it came out as a whisper.

"I think I know what you like."

"How could you possibly?" I was breathless and my tongue darted out to moisten my lips on instinct. The captain's gaze dropped to my mouth and her own lips parted. I squeezed my thighs together, trying to subdue the heat that begged me to open them for her.

"You think I haven't seen you looking at me? The way you blush so sweetly?"

"You look at me too," I retorted and then wished I had kept my mouth shut as whatever predatory thing lurked behind her gaze latched onto my words.

"Indeed, I do." Her gaze left my face and trailed down to where my shirt fell open and exposed the top of my breasts. She licked her lips. "And I think you like it."

Oh lord help me, I did. Something about having her attention on me made me crave it more. I wanted her to look at me. I wanted her to touch me. I wanted her.

I wanted her too much.

"I think…" I stood up from the table, bumping into it as I did and making the wine glasses sway. I had had too much to drink and far too much of the captain's intoxicating attention. I was forgetting myself. I was going to do something foolish if this continued and, if I did, I was not going to be able to stop.

"I believe I ought to retire," I said. My heart was pounding like I had run a mile.

"Is that what you want?"

It was such a dangerous question. A dangerous question from a dangerous woman. One that the look in her eye told me she already knew the answer to.

"I…"

The words would not come.

"Yes?"

The captain rounded the table. Stalking me like I was prey that she would take the time to enjoy. My stomach fluttered until she stood before me. Barely inches between us.

I could not stop myself. I reached out to touch her.

The captain grasped my wrists, backed me into the wall and pinned them above my head with one hand. The other lifted my chin as she tutted.

"All hot and bothered, sweetpea?"

I gasped. It was too much. Too intense. If I even looked at her now, I would lose the scrap of control I still retained over myself. I forced my attention past her to the portrait on the opposite wall but even there, the fearsome expression I had painted her with was now tempting me with its dark, lustful gaze.

"Thinking of painting me again? Maybe you'd like to paint me on those dark nights when you think I don't see you watching." The intensity in her voice made it clear which instance she was referring to. The night I had watched her pleasure herself and been so overcome with lust that I had to relieve my own ache right there and then. My mouth fell open as shame gripped me. She knew I had seen her. She knew what I had done whilst I watched her.

"I—I do not know what you mean." I squirmed but she only held me tighter. If the seas had any mercy, they would have swallowed me up at that moment.

"You know exactly what I mean. You know you touch yourself to the thought of me. Stop denying yourself." Her voice was a low purr that made the hair on the back of my neck prickle and sparked an inferno between my legs. "Look at me."

The captain stepped in even closer, pressing herself against me. The rough material of my shirt rubbed against my nipples as she pushed me harder into the wall. A gasp burst from my lips as the captain's leather clad thigh slipped between my own.

"Would you like me to be the one to grant you that relief?" On the last word, Captain Halliwell ground her leg harder between mine, making me gasp again. Her eyes dropped to my lips.

"How?" My voice was barely above a shaky whisper. I should have been stopping her. I should not have wanted this as much as I did but my traitorous body was already arching to meet her.

The captain hummed, clearly delighted at how desperately I was responding to her.

"I could use my hand…" She tightened her grip on my wrists, then leaned in to whisper in my ear, "I could use my mouth…"

Her tongue darted out to trace my jaw. I moaned and tilted my head to the side to allow her better access. I wanted her mouth all over me.

"But by the look of you, you're half-way there already."

She rotated her hips, her thigh creating such delicious friction in my core that it had me whimpering and balling my hands into fists. I did not care that this was a bad idea. I did not care that she was the last person in the world I should give myself to. Regrets could plague me afterwards if they so wished. But in that moment, I only wanted more.

"Do not stop," I whined as the pressure between my legs was abruptly taken away.

"Begging already?" Captain Halliwell teased, bringing her lips back to my neck. "What will I do with you?"

I was breathless but still managed to lift my chin in challenge. "Whatever you want to."

The captain purred again, low and dangerous. Her hand that was not keeping me captive, slid down my chest, between my breasts, to tug my belt loose. Rough fingertips slid under my shirt to stroke my belly, making me jerk, but the captain's hold on my wrists meant I was going nowhere. It was thrilling how easily she had complete control over me and even more so that she seemed to know exactly what to do with it to make me fall apart completely.

Her fingers trailed their way downwards, into my now open pants and in between my thighs. At a mere touch, my legs shook, and my eyes closed.

"Eyes on me," Captain Halliwell ordered.

"Captain…" I whispered breathlessly as she continued to caress me, sliding lower to dip inside. I did not need her to tell me I was soaking wet.

I gasped and clenched my fists. I wanted to grip her shoulders, entwine my fingers in her hair and kiss her until I was sick of it, touch her like she was touching me. Lord, I wanted to do sinful things to this woman. But my hands remained where she wanted them, pinned to the wall above us.

"Call me Grace," she whispered against my skin as her lips again found my neck, her teeth nipping at my collarbone.

"Grace," I whispered her name and was met with a sharp intake of breath. I said it again. "Grace…"

Her name on my tongue felt as intimate as her touch between my legs. She was 'Grace' to no one but me. Only me. Only now.

Grace was circling now, the pads of her fingertips brushing against my clit. Her touch was heaven, and I whispered her name like a prayer.

"Oh Lord," I moaned.

"Is this how you touch yourself?"

I nodded, biting my lip. "Harder."

"As you wish."

She released my hands to brace herself against the wall and granted my request with relish. I dug my nails into her shoulders as my climax rose within me and sparked a roaring furnace in my core. Stars exploded behind my eyelids. I cried out as I shattered upon her hand, harder than I ever had before.

And then she was gone. Without her holding me, I slid to the floor—my legs jelly-like. She looked down on me and my stomach sank. My Grace was gone. I swallowed as she picked up my blanket from the floor and tossed it to me with a smirk.

I scrambled to rise from the floor on unstable legs, scouring my mind for what could have happened in the last two minutes to banish Grace and bring back the cruel pirate captain who owned that smirk.

"Go to sleep, sweetpea."

"But I…I thought?"

"Thought what?" she scoffed. "That because I'm willing to give you some pleasure that I'll take you to my bed? That we would become lovers?"

"I thought we had something." My voice was small, barely making it past the sudden pain in my chest. We did have something. She was lying to herself if she thought otherwise. Why could she not just admit it?

"Grow up, sweetpea. That was a little mercy to tide you over. As I said when I first decided to spare your life, be grateful for the scraps I deign to throw you."

"You…you are despicable!" I spat, throwing myself into my hammock before she could see the tears threatening to spill.

"I am the captain here. And you are nothing. Don't ever forget it."

Chapter Sixteen

I did not sleep.

The captain's rejection had carved a hole straight through my chest, but it had loosened the ball of rage I kept hidden there. How. Dare. She.

When morning came, I had gone from humiliated, to angry, to furious. I glared at the captain's back as she faced away from me in her bunk.

I stayed until I could stand it no more. I gathered myself and headed to the kitchen early, making sure I slammed the door on my way out. I grinned as I heard her startle and swear. If I was not getting to sleep in, then neither was she.

The dishes were cleaned with a ferocity I did not know I possessed, and even Petra stayed out of my way as I tore about the galley inflicting cleanliness on the tables, benches and floors after I had finished with the crockery. I stewed in my foul mood all day and, by the time I stomped back to the cabin, I knew what I was going to do about it.

The door banged against the wall as I threw it open.

"For goodness' sake!" Captain Halliwell yelled, slamming her quill down. I knew she had been meticulously recording every piece of treasure that had been brought aboard and each crewmember's share. I would not see a single coin of course; I was not part of the crew. Another sour reminder that I did not belong here.

"Sorry, captain," I said primly, closing the door properly this time.

"Get a hold of yourself," she growled.

"Yes, captain." I flipped the lock.

I popped open the top button of my shirt. She desired me and she had been the one to cross this line first. I would be damned if I was not going to wield this new weapon I had been given.

"What are you doing?" Captain Halliwell glanced up as I loosened yet another button.

"According to you? Absolutely nothing at all," I said scathingly, sliding my now half-buttoned shirt off one shoulder.

The captain's gaze hardened as I swayed around her desk.

"You should watch how you speak to me."

"No, captain," I snarled, grabbing the chair and dragging it back so that I could straddle the captain's legs. "You should watch how you speak to me."

I was drunk on my anger. Drunk and reckless. All my life, I had been meek. I had done as I was told and shoved my feelings down and where had it gotten me? Here. On this godforsaken ship being bullied and tormented only to be bartered away for a ransom. Just as I was to be bartered away into marriage.

I may have been a captive on this ship, but I had been a prisoner my whole life and I was sick of it. I had been granted a brief reprieve with Madame, thinking I could maybe make a life for myself, maybe I could do what I wanted for a change, maybe I did not have to be what someone else made me into. But what was I there but yet another meek little girl? In my frustration at the captain, my thoughts had become dangerously close to piercing that thick wall I had built around a truth I was too scared to admit. That for all my dreams of a future with her, Madame would have never seen me as an equal. I was a precious pearl for her to treasure, but an object nonetheless. One that could be cast aside.

"What the hell do you think—?"

The captain's angry question was cut off as I batted her tricorn hat from her head.

"Captain or not, you do not get to play with me and then cast me aside like I am nothing."

Captain Halliwell's eyes were wide with shock, and she started to say something, but I gripped a fistful of her shirt. The simple action sent a ripple through me.

"Think carefully about what you wish to say, *captain*. I know my worth. I know what I gave to you last night and I know how you feel about me," I hissed. "You want to dominate me? Fine. But do not dare disrespect me."

The captain's throat bobbed as she swallowed hard. Her lips parted. I had intended that to be the end of my speech, but the black of her pupils engulfed any brown in her eyes as they darted to my lips. I had expected her to be angry when I said my piece and I could tell that, somewhere inside, she was. But she was not nearly as angry as she was aroused. The realization made something hidden rear up within me. I felt powerful. I *was* powerful. She wanted me. She craved me. The truth was written across her face. But I would not damn well make myself small anymore. Well, if she wanted me, then she could have me. All of me, including the dark little parts of me I had hidden for so long. I was done being meek.

"You...you like this, do you not? You like being played with as much as you like to play." I let my fingers trail to her throat as I ground my hips into her, relishing her groan. Her pulse was hammering under my touch. I leaned in to kiss the captain's jaw and whispered in a low rasp, "If I were to reach into your pants right now, would you be wet for me?"

The coarse words were unfamiliar on my tongue, but delicious nonetheless. An exotic delicacy. Captain Halliwell's breath caught.

I nipped at her earlobe. A tiny gasp escaped her.

"When I ask you a question, *Grace*, I expect an

answer," I growled as I leaned back and tightened my grip on her neck. Oh lord, I was enjoying this. I had always known I would, but this was my first time letting myself completely loose. My first time taking charge. I may have been the one teasing the pirate captain, but I could feel the ache of my own arousal building between my legs as she gazed up at me with widened eyes.

"I asked you," I repeated, "are you wet for me right now?"

"Yes," Grace rasped, heat coloring her tanned cheeks. The scratches I had given her had not been deep and were already faded to pale pink. A part of me wished they would never fade. That my mark would remain on her long after she had forgotten me.

I smiled. "Good."

I released my hold to trail down Grace's throat to her collarbone and to the laces at the front of her shirt. I loosened the first knot.

"What—?"

Her question was silenced as I pressed a finger to her lips and shushed her.

"Out there, you may be captain. In here, right now, just be mine."

Grace nodded, her eyes never wavering from my face.

With the laces of her shirt loosened, all it took was a quick jerk to have the captain's breasts spilling forth. *Magnificent.* I almost whispered it aloud, but I stopped myself. She did not deserve my compliments right now. Her nipples were hard and peaked under my hands, growing stiffer as I rolled them between my thumb and forefinger. From the way she pressed herself up to meet my touch, her nipples were just as sensitive as mine.

"Do you like me touching you, Grace?"

The woman beneath me moaned her agreement,

biting down on her lower lip and tipping her head back as I pinched and then massaged her breasts. They filled my hands as if they were made for them. Her moans reached an almost guttural tone when I lowered my head to capture one of her stiff buds in my mouth. I circled it with my tongue, sucking gently, while continuing to grope the soft mounds. Grace was about to learn that my tutor taught me far more than art and that I was a very attentive student.

The captain's hips rolled underneath me, trying to grind, to gain some friction, some release that I was not ready to give her.

Sucking hard, I sank my teeth in and was rewarded by a small yelp from the captain. I let out a heady groan at the sound. It was so unlike anything I had heard from her before. It was uncontrolled and raw. I craved more. I wanted to hear all of the sounds I could drag from her. I wanted to hear exactly what my touch made her feel.

I gripped her waist to keep her still and sat back to admire the mark I had left. A small circle of reddish-purple in the shape of my mouth marred the perfect curve of the captain's breast.

"Did you just bite me, you fiend?" Grace gasped, her hands going to her now overly sensitive breasts.

I caught her hands and guided them away from her breasts to the arms of the chair where I held them down firmly before once again wrapping my fingers around the captain's neck, forcing her to tip her head back.

"No touching. It is my turn to enjoy you."

Grace let out a moan at my words, once more biting down on her lip as if trying to keep it in. I could see her struggle etched across her face. Her pride against her pleasure.

I unbuckled the captain's belt and left her lap to sink to my knees before her chair before her pride could rob me of my enjoyment.

"Lift your hips," I commanded.

She complied and I eased her pants down her muscular legs, taking the opportunity to run my hands over the woman's powerful thighs. Goosebumps sprang up in the wake of my touch. I pushed Grace's knees apart.

"My, my," I teased as I ran a finger along the damp insides of her thighs. "Is all this for me?"

By now, Grace's breath was coming in pants, and she nodded helplessly as I continued to caress her so close to her intimate parts. I slapped her thigh.

"I asked you a question, Grace."

"Yes," she gasped. "Yes, damn it, it's for you."

I planted a kiss on the inside of her knee and then another. Moving ever closer to where the captain really wanted my mouth to be. Again, Grace rolled her hips, seeking contact but I held her firmly, still leisurely kissing. To be the one teasing instead of being teased for once was addictive. Perhaps knocking Grace's pride down a peg would be dangerous for my own ego with how much she was squirming and moaning for me, but I loved it, and I knew I would have found myself dripping if I dipped into my own pants.

I dragged my nails down her thighs, eliciting a rasping groan from her. The sound had barely tailed off when I leaned in to swipe my tongue through the captain's wet folds. Hot, wet and salty like the sea, I dipped back in for another taste. The captain's legs shuddered as I licked slowly and deliberately until I reached that sensitive little bud at the top. I flicked my tongue against it, relishing in the wave of tremors that it produced. I alternated between slow and fast, glancing up with a grin to see Grace's white knuckled grip on the arms of the chair. I dragged my teeth cruelly across her clit and grinned at her whine.

My ferocious captain, indeed.

I gave one more long, slow lick along her slit. "You have to tell me what you want."

The warring emotions on the captain's face were

delicious but nothing compared to the words that eventually spilled from her mouth.

"Fuck me," she gasped. "Sweetpea…please."

Oh, what those words did to me.

"If you insist." I grinned as I planted another kiss on the captain's trembling thigh.

Two fingers slipped easily through her slick heat and when I curled them, Grace let out a keening groan. I pumped them in and out as I returned my mouth to that sweet spot. In that moment, I was a musician and she was my favorite instrument.

"Oh yes…" Grace's hands found my head and her finger's tangled in my hair as I continued. "Oh, sweetpea."

Muscles clenched around my fingers as I fucked her harder. Grace's moans became grunts to the rhythm of my movements. Her release was almost mine. Taking the captain's clit into my mouth, I sucked hard.

Grace fell apart.

Her powerful thighs clamped around my head like a vice as her climax tore through her. When her legs finally relaxed, shuddering with the final waves of her release, she whimpered as I withdrew my fingers from her.

Rising from my knees, I looked down on my captain as I adjusted my own clothing. Her bare breasts heaved, and her head was tipped back, eyes closed. Slumped back in her chair, her legs remained wide open and her thighs glistened.

I was barely tousled as I stood over her and she…She was a beautiful mess. A beautiful mess of my making.

I leaned in and cleaned my fingers off on her open shirt.

"What…?" Grace mumbled.

I kissed her. Locking our lips together and sliding my tongue into the captain's unresisting mouth so that she could taste her own pleasure. When Grace reached for me to continue the kiss, I pulled back and gripped her jaw hard.

"Never call me nothing again." I straightened up and tossed my hair over my shoulder. "I require some air."

I left the captain, half-naked and splayed open, still dazed from her orgasm, and stepped out into the cool, starlit night.

I knew when she had finally pulled herself together and come to find me when the cool scents of the night became infused with citrus, spice and sex.

The captain cleared her throat. I turned just enough to raise my eyebrows at her.

"Well, you certainly know how to make your point. You surprise me, sweetpea."

She leaned her elbows on the railing beside where I had been staring out across the dark sea.

"I am not above admitting when I am wrong." She swallowed. "And I was wrong. My position is precarious. I'm sure you have noticed. I cannot give the crew any reasons to doubt me. To think I'm weak. I cannot have them see that I'm going…hell, that I've already gone soft for you. It's dangerous for me and for you."

"Then, like I said, be the captain you need to be out here." I slipped my hand in hers. "But in private? For the rest of the time we have together? You are mine, Grace."

Chapter Seventeen

I had never imagined this misadventure happening to me, but in the calm moments of salty sea air during the day or the heat-filled passion that filled my nights, I started to daydream of this becoming my life. Of course, I still hated the hard labor I was forced to do, and I would have killed for a proper bath, but for all that I was trapped aboard the Bone Heart, I had never felt so liberated. As the lowest ranking member on board, there were no expectations of me. I had to follow orders and complete my tasks, but I never had to perform. I had come to the realization that my whole life had been a performance for an audience of my father's choosing. An audition for a part I never wanted to play. How could I return to society after this? Maybe I truly would need to take time to recover in the countryside.

I had given up hope of ever reuniting with Madame Chevalier much more easily than I had thought possible. When I was finally returned home to Beauris, I would have scarce opportunity or means to make my way to Mulla. Unless she also returned to Beauris, I would not see her again. I had also decided that that was for the best. My time with her, however all-encompassing it may have been, had passed. That too, had been a part to play. Once I realized that I had never even once called her by her given name, it was as if my eyes had finally been opened. She would have always been Madame and I, her pearl. What we had had not been real. When I finally saw our relationship for what it was, it was as if a weight had lifted from my shoulders.

I paused to wipe sweat from my brow. Grace had taken the time that morning to comb my salt-stiffened locks and tie my hair back with a ribbon so that it would stay out of my way while I worked. It was a far cry from my usual, carefully styled hair that was never held together by less than ten pins. She had also gifted me a battered, old, brown version of her tricorn hat to protect me from the glare of the sun, and I took a moment to fan myself with it. With the hat, loose trousers and patched shirt I wore, I looked every part the pirate. I had even gone barefoot today. We had indeed sailed southwards and the heat was building by the day.

I had just slapped my hat back on my head and was about to get back to scrubbing the deck when the shouts rang out. Sails on the horizon. I abandoned my task to squint in the midday sun at the distant smudge. I knew if we had been alone, I could have asked Grace to lend me her spyglass so that I could see but, with the crew around there was no chance of that.

The only person who knew what we had been doing was Petra. She had walked in on us one day when Grace had snuck me away from my kitchen duties for a secret dalliance in the cargo hold. The cook had come looking for me ready to scold me for slacking but had found me very much not slacking between the captain's thighs. She had backed out of the hold without a word. When I had returned to the galley half an hour later, red-faced and sheepish she had given me a mountain of work to do and stalked off to have words with the captain. Grace told me later that Petra had given her an earful about what was appropriate for a captain and about the dangers of becoming distracted.

I quite enjoyed that she was so distracted by me, but Grace had said she was right. We had to be careful, and the crew would not be as understanding about her 'going soft' as she put it.

Petra had pulled me aside more than once since then

and warned me to keep my mouth shut if I knew what was good for me and to stop gazing at the captain like a lovesick fool. Occasionally her rebukes were accompanied by a swat about the ear if I dared roll my eyes at her.

I caught the captain's eye as she strode across the deck, but she simply jerked her head back to my abandoned bucket and mop. I held back a chuckle. Ever the stern captain in front of her men. She was not nearly so stern when she was holding back screams of pleasure last night or when she backed me against the door to the cabin to give me one last searing kiss before we started our day. I let myself smile. The secrecy of our affair made it all the more exciting.

"They could've followed us."

The concern in Ramsden's voice caught my attention. Of course, the Bone Heart was carrying a wealth of treasure that, in Grace's words, any pirate worth his salt would think about taking for himself, but no one should have known what was concealed down below the Heart's decks. Not even all of the crew had known the nature of their voyage when it began. Rumors of a treasure hunt had a habit of becoming bloody.

Captain Halliwell's expression darkened. "Eyes sharp. I want to know the second they change course."

The next half hour was tense but, after a while, there was no mistaking it. The ship was headed right for us.

"It looks like the Salted Lady, cap'n!"

The captain swore.

"Battle stations!" she bellowed.

"What is happening?" I asked, wringing my hands as the crew leapt into action.

Grace's mouth was a grim line. "Get to the cabin. Now."

With all the time I had spent in the captain's quarters, I thought I knew every inch of them. As it turned out, Grace had kept a few secrets to herself. A push of her hand against an inconspicuous-looking panel on the wall had it swinging out to reveal a small space behind.

"Get in."

I beg your pardon?" I yelped in alarm. I was not a large woman but, even so, that was far too small a space for me. It seemed my opinion mattered not, however, and the captain had me bundled in before I could make a decent protest. The wooden panels pressed into my shoulders on either side, and I had to duck my head slightly to fit.

"Someone must have told them about the treasure. They let us do the hard part and now they're coming to collect," Grace spat before her gaze softened and she squeezed my hand. "The Salted Lady is not known for her mercy. Stay here."

Muffled voices bellowed from all parts of the ship; their words lost but their urgency clear. The first roars of cannon fire made us both brace ourselves, but they did not land. Warning shots. We would not be given any more.

"That was cannon fire! Actual cannon fire! This is madness," I cried.

"Madness would be you getting involved in the fire fight that is about to happen. This is not the time to argue." Grace planted her palm on my chest to stop me from wriggling out of my hiding space. "Listen to me, sweetpea. The Bone Heart is out-gunned. They will not want to sink us, but there's a good chance that they'll board us. You stay here and you do not make a sound until I come get you. Is that understood?"

The blazing fire in her eyes left no room for negotiation.

"Yes, captain." I whispered, shrinking back into the cupboard as the reality the situation dawned on me. This was no mere scuffle. Oh lord, people were going to die.

She reached up to cup my cheek as I stared at her, eyes wide with the terror that was starting to grip my bones. Her voice softened. "Promise me you will stay hidden."

"I promise."

She pushed a pistol into my hands.

I cannot! I will not!" I protested. "Grace, I could never shoot someone!"

"That's not what this is for." Her eyes were fathomless, black holes as she adjusted the pistol in my hands.

My breath stuttered and my heart leapt into my throat as she pressed the barrel into the soft skin underneath my chin.

"If we lose this battle…if I…if I do not return…" She took a shuddering breath. "You do not want to be alive for what they will do when they find you."

My mouth fell open as I gaped at her. Her lips pressed into a hard line and a muscle in her jaw twitched. Fear pooled in my belly and clawed up my spine. Captain Grace Halliwell was scared.

"Be brave," was all she said as she pressed her lips to my brow and slid the panel closed with a final click.

It was much like being back in the chest I had been smuggled aboard in almost a month ago, although this compartment was infinitely less comfortable with its lack of cushioning. I ached to stretch my legs out, but I was terrified to move. I held the pistol as I would a venomous snake. I knew Grace was deadly serious about how to use it, but I knew in my heart I would not be able to. I could only hope that if it came to that, she would not be around to see whatever happened to me.

I do not know how long I was in the hidden compartment before the other ship caught up with us. Sounds were muffled in my hiding space, and I could not always tell where they were coming from, but I recognized the sound of rifles when they started firing. A moment's quiet followed the shots before something huge and heavy crashed into the side of the ship and I slammed against the walls of the compartment, making me grateful that I had Grace's hat to cushion my head.

And then, all hell broke loose.

Gunshots, screams, the thud of falling bodies and the clash of swords echoed around my tiny space. Any one of the crew could be injured or dying. I ached to open the door and see for myself. Not knowing was torturous, but the risk of being shot myself kept me rooted to the spot. I did not know how to defend myself, let alone offer aid.

The crew must have been putting up a decent fight against the other pirates, I thought, as the sounds of fighting continued. That meant they were alive. That their captain had not yet fallen.

If I had not been straining to hear every sound, I might have missed the footsteps. Heavy footsteps. Too heavy to be Grace. Inside the cabin.

Something knocked lightly against the wall to my far right. A step. Another knock. My heart forgot how to beat properly and leapt around my chest like a wild beast. Someone was checking the panels for hidden compartments.

I was not being quiet. Fear-filled whimpers forced their way up my throat, and I pressed my free hand over my mouth. They were going to find me. I clutched Grace's pistol in my sweaty grip.

Light flooded the cramped space as the panel was slid back. With a squeak, I brandished the pistol wildly, squinting in the brightness.

"What're you doing with a thing like that?" I was relieved of my weapon instantly.

"Marcos?" I was lightheaded with relief at the sight of the red-haired pirate as he tucked the pistol safely into his waistband. "Lord, I thought you were one of them. Did the captain send you? What is happening?"

I half-tumbled out of my hiding place, clutching onto his shirt to steady myself. A muscular arm went around my back.

I peeked around him. The clashing of swords and

raucous battle cries were louder now that I was not sequestered away in my hidey hole.

"They are still fighting! What are you doing in here?"

His arms around me suddenly felt far more restrictive than they had a second ago.

"The captain said I was to hide until she came for me." I extricated myself from his arms but there was nowhere to go.

"She's busy."

As I took a step back, he matched it until my back pressed against the wall.

"What are you doing?"

He planted his hands on either side of me, barring my way out. "Captain ain't coming. We've got a little time to ourselves."

"The whole crew could be dying out there!"

I reckon some of them will be." He gave me a horrible grin. "Not me though. I'll surrender, become part of the new crew. A ship like the Lady always needs extra hands. And not you. No, they won't kill you. Not yet anyway. And I don't want to waste an opportunity to get the first taste."

I did not get a chance to process my horror at his words before he was on me, his mouth slavering down the side of my neck and his grubby hands scrabbling at my shirt. Pushing with all my might did nothing to dislodge him. He chuckled at my efforts.

"Grace! GRACE!" I screamed.

"She ain't coming," he growled, trying to wedge his knee between my thighs to force them open.

In a panicked moment of ferocity, I leaned in and clamped my teeth down on his carlobc as hard as I could.

He yelled in pain and shock before his expression turned murderous and, before I could skirt around him and flee for the door, he threw me to the ground. I tried my best to scramble away despite the pain radiating up my spine from the impact, but he was on me again, one hand around my throat. I clawed at his hand as he resumed trying to force his way in between my legs.

Hot blood from his torn ear rained down on my face. It was in my eyes, in my mouth. Choking me. Drowning me. I thrashed, trying to wriggle out from underneath him, and that is when I saw it. The captain's pistol was tucked into his waistband. With a strangled cry, I seized it and yanked it free. His eyes widened and he grabbed for the pistol right as I jammed it under his chin and squeezed the trigger.

The shot was deafening, and smoke stabbed at my eyes but when it cleared, my stomach lurched. Marcos was still leering down at me.

"You little bitch," he spat. "You'll pay for that."

He had managed to smack the gun away and the bullet had missed him by a half foot. With the pistol now lying halfway across the cabin, I realized with a horrible clarity that had lost my only chance at fighting him off. He was too big and too strong for me to stop him. He was going to do this. A sob wracked through me and I closed my eyes. I could not escape this.

Just as I resigned myself to my fate, the door flew open with such force I thought it must have been more cannon fire.

The air dripped with deadly silence. Outside, the fighting had stopped.

Marcos froze above me, and I twisted to see the silhouetted outline of Captain Halliwell in the doorway. The cutlass in her hand dripped blood and she had murder in her eyes. I had never seen anything so glorious as her face twisted into a snarl.

"Get your fucking hands off her."

Chapter Eighteen

I refused to look at what was strewn across the deck as I exited the cabin in a daze. Two of the Bone Heart's crew held Marcos' arms as they dragged him out into the daylight. Others sat, stood and leaned, sporting bloodied bandages. I knew their faces but not their names. A huddle of the enemy crew was in the middle of the deck on their knees with their hands raised.

The captain strode ahead of us all, head held high and bellowed for attention. She was splattered with blood, and she was favoring her right leg as she walked. Was she hurt? I wanted to go to her, ensure that she was unharmed, but my limbs were not moving as I wished them to, and I ended up sitting down instead.

I did not know how much time had passed since Grace had found me. Saved me. I had someone's coat draped over my shoulders, and the taste of rum lingered on my tongue from a hip flask that had found its way into my hands.

"What's going on?" Petra hollered across the deck. Blood dripped from her hairline, but she appeared otherwise unscathed. She held a meat cleaver in her fist.

"I'll tell you what's going on," Grace said with a glint in her eye. "While we were fighting for our lives, Marcos decided to go after the stowaway."

"He did what?" Petra dropped her cleaver and was next to me in an instant, squeezing my hand. "Girl, did he hurt you?"

"Tried to," I mumbled as she pawed at me, checking

for wounds. "I am unharmed."

"Getting his cock wet was more important to him than your lives!" Grace roared, pointing at Marcos with her sword. "More important than your coin!"

She turned, her fury gone from her face in an instant as she bore down on the pirate and instead adopted an almost sweet tone of voice. "Let's see it then."

Marcos' face went slack. "Captain?"

"I said," Grace sneered, grasping his belt, "Let us see the pathetic worm that was more important than fighting beside your crewmates."

She yanked his belt open with an almost careless flick of her wrist. I caught a glimpse of his pale, hairy legs and looked away. I knew in theory what was between them, but that did not mean I needed to see it.

Grace's laugh was almost deranged as it rang out across the deck. "Well, I certainly do not think that is worth very much at all."

She turned to the bloodied crew of the Bone Heart.

"Any of you, is that worth more than the sacks full of gold we get when we return the stowaway unharmed? Worth more than your lives"?"

No one answered but the air thickened with contempt.

"Hm," the captain said shrewdly. "Ramsden. As first mate, do you think that is worth more than your life? More than any of our lives? Would you betray your crew for that?"

Ramsden looked down on Marcos in disgust and spat on the deck.

Murmurs of discontent growled from all sides. The words "traitor" and "coward" flickered through the air.

"That's what I thought."

Grace lifted her pistol and fired.

I almost wished she had just shot him in the head. Marcos' agonized howls were louder than the cannon fire had been. He was still screaming when the pirates pitched him over the side of the ship as unforgiving as the sea that claimed him.

Until that point, I had managed to control myself as the blood soaked into the deck that I had so diligently scrubbed that morning. I doubled over and heaved. I had never had a particularly strong constitution.

When I was done emptying my stomach, Grace took me by the shoulders and guided me back to the cabin. I thought she would say something. Offer some word of comfort. She did not. She left immediately. I could hear her bellowing orders, but the words entered my mind in a jumble. Petra appeared with a steaming cup of tea and pressed me into drinking it, but she too was needed on deck.

I was alone for hours.

I curled up in the captain's bunk. It felt sturdier than my hammock. Her pistol lay beside me. I did not know why I had picked it up since I did not know how to reload it. I just wanted to have it.

When Grace finally did come back, the skies were darkening. She instinctively looked for me in my hammock. The flash of panic across her features when she did not immediately see me should have brought me some comfort. It did not.

If she minded me being in her bunk, she did not make it known as she shucked off her bloodied clothing and sat down in just her undergarments. I moved my feet to give her more space.

For a long time, she did not say a word.

"Tomorrow, we set course for the Cinerian Islands. I'll send word ahead to arrange a meeting time and place. It's close enough to Beauris and it's time I sent you home. The Bone Heart is no place for you."

I nodded numbly.

The thought of going home should have filled me

with joy, especially after today.

"I…" Grace cleared her throat.

I waited but she simply shook her head. "You can take the bunk."

She stood and went to her chair.

"We could share," I blurted.

Her eyebrows rose.

"Please. I do not…I need…" I sniffled, tears spilled down my cheeks. "Will you hold me?"

I felt like a child begging for comfort, but Grace had crossed the cabin and swept me into her arms before I could regret saying anything. It was a tight fit for both of us to squeeze into the narrow bunk, but Grace uttered no word of complaint. She held me as my shoulders shook in silent sobs that soaked her front.

"I should have protected you better," she murmured into my hair. "I'm so sorry, Elise."

Chapter Nineteen

I should have been angry when Grace locked me in her cabin to go ashore a few days later, but she had kissed me so sweetly goodbye that I could not find much more than mild annoyance. She had promised to not dally and to return to me quickly— she only needed to organize my return home and pick up some sorely needed supplies. Besides, if I was locked in, then it meant that everyone else was locked out and that suited me quite well after Marcos' attack. Whispers had been flying that he had conspired with the Salted Lady since before the Bone Heart had even started her treasure hunt. Someone had certainly talked, that was for sure.

Even with the added safety of the cabin locks, I would have preferred going ashore with my captain. I longed for solid ground, a change of scenery but, most of all, I felt safest by her side. After Marcos, she had sworn to me that no one would lay a finger on me again. Over and over, she had sworn as she kissed my forehead, my cheeks, my palms.

I watched the rowboat from the window until it landed on the sandy shore and the figures aboard were nothing more than smudges. Grace still would not tell me where we were lest I let it slip back in Beauris. I wondered idly what kind of hideout she had on this island. A dripping cave filled with treasure and old bones, perhaps. Or maybe ancient chests filled with gold were buried in the sand.

I sketched while I waited for her return. She had allowed me some ink and parchment of my own with the condition that I drew her at least once more before I left. I did not know how long I had left on this ship, so I had been putting off starting it. I did not want to think about leaving. Leaving the Bone Heart meant leaving Grace, and I was not ready to admit that yet. My efforts were instead focused on shading a small drawing of the cabin interior that I had come to think of as home.

The captain did not return until late in the day and she looked exhausted as she swept into the cabin.

"Your father has agreed to the terms," she stated without preamble. "I sent the details of time and place. We'll be in the Cinerian Isles in ten days if the winds are favorable."

"I see," I replied. Ten days. I would be on my way home in ten days. I knew Grace felt awful that harm had almost come to me under her care and that was why she was so intent on getting me home sooner rather than later. I did wish that she wanted to keep me a little longer, though.

"What's the matter, love?" she asked, coming to my side and kissing the top of my head. "I thought you'd be happy."

She still called me 'sweetpea' sometimes— especially in in front of others— and, although I did not mind it nearly as much as I used to, I adored the new name she had gifted me. It did not mean that she loved me, of course. Love was not something that the world would let us have, and we both knew that. But it did not stop my insides from warming and my belly from fluttering whenever she called me her love.

"I am, I am," I reassured her with a smile and then changed the subject. I did not want to examine the reasons for my melancholy. "If that is all sorted, then what of you? You have your treasure now. What next?"

"There's never enough treasure, love. Plus, you are thinking of the gold. But that was not the only thing we brought up from that wreck. We found maps. Maps that no one has seen in centuries. That was the real treasure.

I'll spruce up the ship, rustle up some extra crew

members..." She exhaled as she stretched. Her eyes had taken on that sparkle they always had when she spoke of exploration. "...and then the Bone Heart will be off for new worlds. I will be a great adventurer and I will make that name for myself."

"Grace Halliwell, adventurer," I mused. "I think I prefer you as a pirate."

Whatever Grace was about to reply was interrupted by a loud growl from my stomach.

"It seems I have neglected you yet again," she said as she glanced at the darkened skies outside the window. "Dinner won't be for a while I'm afraid, but it'll be worth the wait. I will fetch it for you when it's ready."

"Must I really stay in here?" I gave her my finest pleading look that should have melted stone. "I have been shut up in this cabin all day, you know."

"Yes, you really must, I'm afraid. We set sail first thing in the morning and then you may roam the ship as you please. But I cannot have my captive on deck while we are docked. I trust you not to leap overboard but my crew will not be of the same mind."

I muttered my complaints under my breath.

She grinned as she fished something round from her pocket and tossed it in the air. "Something to tide you over in the meantime."

Grace sat on her bunk and gestured for me to join her. When I went to sit at her side, she shifted and grabbed my hips and angled me so that I sat on her lap instead. Perhaps I did not mind staying in the cabin too much after all, I thought with a grin.

She used her dagger to cut a slice from the apple and held it to my lips. I lifted my hand to take it, but she tutted and held it out of my reach.

"Open your mouth."

I raised my eyebrows at her but did as she asked and

let her feed me, moaning in delight at my first taste of fresh fruit in far too long. I ate in silence until the last sweet slice which, instead of feeding to me by hand, the captain held between her own teeth and lowered her mouth to mine. As I took it, our lips brushed in the briefest of apple flavored kisses.

Grace's hands roamed my thighs as I swallowed the last of the fruit. I was so tempted to give in to my body's desires and let her continue but, in the long hours I had to think that day, I had decided what I wanted.

"If I am to remain here even longer, the least you could do is provide entertainment."

"What kind of entertainment would you like, love?" the captain asked, her eyes locked to my lips as I licked juice from them.

"Not that kind," I laughed. "I want your story. I want to know more about you. Who you really are when you are not 'Captain Halliwell'."

"There's not much to tell. Would you not rather I used my mouth for something else?"

"You are changing the subject. I will not allow myself to be distracted this time," I said with reproach, twisting around so that I straddled her lap. "You know everything about me."

Grace sighed. "It is not a happy story, sweetpea. Whatever narrative you have created in your head of my past, I can assure you that you will be disappointed. I was never a good person."

"Tell me," I insisted. "I will have all of you, the good and the bad."

Grace studied my earnest expression for a moment.

"What would you like to know?"

"Where are you from? Do you have family? You mentioned your nana. Is she still with us?" I bit my lip to stop the rest of my questions from tumbling out.

Grace let out an exaggerated groan, but it seemed my pouting did have power over her after all.

"I was born in Castar, a small town on the mainland but far farther west than Beauris. My family were in the fabric business. My nana was a seamstress and took commissions from the ladies of the town." Grace's fingers traced mindless patterns on my thighs as she spoke. "She died some ten years past."

"I was never happy with my lot in life and always wanted more. I wanted to make a name for myself. I…" Grace trailed off and cleared her throat. "I did some bad things. I lied. I stole. That's actually how I met the lover I spoke of. Rosemary was her name. She was one of my nana's clients and she caught me looking through her things while she was being fitted for a new gown."

"How ever did common thievery become romance?" I asked, wrinkling my nose.

Grace laughed. "I asked myself that many times. She said she saw something intriguing in me."

"You are intriguing," I murmured, toying with the laces of her shirt and winding them around my finger. "Then what happened?"

"We met in secret for many months. Rosemary offered to provide for me, but I declined. I was too proud. I gave her many gifts that I couldn't afford to prove that I didn't need providing for. I even gave her my nana's emerald ring. I burned bridges trying to keep her."

"Did you try to find her again? After her husband tried to kill you and you became a pirate?"

"I did but, when the Bone Heart next returned to Castar, years had passed. I could find no trace of Rosemary, and my nana had been long buried. I found my family's shop running under a different name. No one could tell me what became of the previous owners other than heartbreak had ruined them." A haunted look flashed across Grace's face. "I ruined them."

"They must have thought you had died," I whispered in horror. The words 'it wasn't your fault' were on the tip of my tongue but Grace shook her head as if knowing what I was about to say.

"They never knew what became of me, although I doubt they would have taken any pride in having a pirate for a daughter."

"A pirate captain"," I corrected.

"Indeed." Grace's smile did not reach her eyes. "I told you I am not a good person. I never was and I never will be. The sooner you leave this ship and forget me, the better. I would ruin you, love."

The ghost of tears glistened at the corners of her dark eyes, bitter regret etched in every line of her face. She looked away from me. If she thought I would think less of her now that I knew the shame of her past, she was mistaken. I would think less of her were she not ashamed. She was no saint, that was true. But nor was she rotten. Whatever she was, for now, she was mine.

A gasp escaped her as my lips collided with hers. I let my tongue slide over hers, washing away the bitterness of her regrets with the taste of apple that lingered in my mouth. My fingers entwined in her hair as I bore us back onto the bunk.

"What sweet ruination that would be."

Chapter Twenty

Setting foot on solid ground again was bliss. I almost asked Grace for a moment to jump down from the pier to the beach to dig my hands through the soft sand underneath, but she had cautioned me against doing anything conspicuous. I clung to her side as she strode with an air of confidence across the docks and through the port. The air was filled with the scent of salt, fish and sailors' sweat but, now and again, the aroma of exotic spices reached my nose as other ships unloaded their wares.

The crew had begrudged that the captain only gave them a small portion of their share in the treasure to spend ashore, but she had argued that any more would bring attention and make the Bone Heart and its crew a target for thieves. Besides, they would not be staying long. This was only a small detour to drop me off, get the ransom and they would be back on the high seas as soon as possible.

The bulk of the treasure, plus what the crew had raided from the Salted Lady before she was laid to rest on the sea floor, would be taken to ports farther south where the haggling was more profitable. The Bone Heart had taken on a few extra crew members from the conquered ship and new faces mingled with those I already knew as we took to shore. I had not inquired but I assumed the rest of the Lady's crew now rested with her in the depths.

I felt oddly forlorn as I looked back at the ship. It was easily one of the largest ships in the harbor and, although her off-white sails were furled away, I knew that they would be nothing more than clouds on the horizon soon enough. Her customary black flag was also hidden below deck in favor of a cheerful sky-blue one that waved us goodbye from her mast. I had mixed feelings about leaving the Bone Heart. On one hand, I could have skipped for joy at the thought of never washing a dish again, but the personal freedom that life at sea had given me was going to be hard to give up.

As if sensing my sudden gloom, Grace nudged me with her elbow and pointed up ahead to a two-story building just past the port district.

"We'll stay the night here. Just us. The rest will go farther into town for accommodation that offers…entertainment. I'm friendly with the owner here and it's one of the only places on this damn island that won't give you bedbugs." She grinned at me, but I only managed a weak smile in return. "They also have the best cook."

That did cheer me up. Petra did her best but, without many ingredients, our meals had become grim at best.

"I could eat," I replied, quickening my pace.

At the thought of food, my stomach had awakened and had begun to growl by the time we entered the inn.

I had assumed the owner would be a man but, to my surprise as we ducked through the low door, it was a fair-haired woman who shrieked a greeting and yanked Grace into a tight embrace. Something twinged in me at their familiarity.

The woman peppered Grace with questions about how long she would be staying and if she had been keeping well. I tried to ignore the way her breasts almost spilled from her tight bodice.

"Will you be staying the night?" The woman all but purred the question and her gaze roamed the captain's body suggestively.

I cleared my throat. Loudly.

"Aye. We will be staying." Grace grinned at my expression. "Sweetpea, this is my good friend, Maria."

"A pleasure," I said politely.

"Likewise," she said equally polite.

I had learned from my mother that manners could be a much more effective weapon than harsh words and, from the way Maria's fingertips lingered on Grace's arm, I very much wished for a weapon.

"A charming establishment you have, Miss Maria. Such...interesting choices in décor." I glanced up at the fishing nets hung from the ceiling and the rows of decorative jugs that lined shelves along the back wall.

"We'll take a room with a bath please, Maria, and some food."

"Of course," Maria replied smoothly, gracing the captain with a smile and me with a curious glance. "Take a table and I'll bring it out for you. Ale?"

"Oh, you know me better than that," Grace chided.

Maria grinned. "Wine it is."

She smiled once more and disappeared through a swinging door. I did not miss that she deliberately rocked her hips as she walked away.

A sharp slap to my backside had me hissing and glaring at the captain.

"I said inconspicuous, love. Be nice."

"I was perfectly nice," I growled back as she steered us to a table.

I was sure Grace was going to scold me some more, but a carafe of wine appeared almost instantly and she poured us both a generous glass.

"Ah, that's the stuff. Maria's wine cellar is also the best in all the Cinerian Isles."

I must have scowled because she reached over to pinch my cheek.

"So adorable when you're angry."

I slapped her hand away. "I would not be angry if you did not bring me to your former lover's establishment."

That had the captain roaring with laughter.

"Oh sweetpea. Maria and I have never been intimate. She may be a shameless flirt, but that's purely business. She likes men."

"Oh."

"Yes 'oh'." Grace shook her head. "So be nice."

"You hardly dissuaded my assumption!" I said indignantly.

I was saved from replying by the arrival of two steaming bowls of some kind of spicy smelling stew.

"Enjoy," Maria said as she set the bowls down. "It's my own recipe."

"Thank you, Maria," I granted her my most genuine smile, ashamed that I had judged her so harshly. "It looks wonderful."

I groaned in delight at the first spoonful.

"As much as I enjoy it, I did not expect jealousy from you, sweetpea. Is that not unbecoming of a lady?" Grace said, cocking her head to the side with a grin. She was mocking me.

"Brute," I muttered into my wine glass.

"I'll make it up to you."

Her smirk was downright sinful and sent a shiver down my spine.

Chapter Twenty One

I moaned in utter delight as I sunk into the warm water. I had forgotten that Grace had ordered a bath in our room and, when we ventured upstairs to our accommodations, I had squealed in delight.

"I am never leaving this tub," I declared.

"Then you'll miss out on all the benefits of having a real bed," Grace teased. I had been so eager to bathe that I had been undressed and in the water before she even had her boots off.

I opened my eyes.

"You have convinced me."

The captain laughed.

"Let's clean up first, shall we?"

She picked up the sponge and lathered it up with soap, taking her time to drag it over every inch of me.

"Join me," I whispered.

She did not need asking twice and stripped off, slipping into the tub with me. I scrubbed her down with the sponge, paying extra attention to my favorite parts of her body and loving how my hands slipped so smoothly over her skin.

The bath was small for both of us, but I hardly minded being pressed up against her wet, soapy body. She was at my back with her legs on either side of me as she washed my hair.

I tipped my head back against her chest as her fingers trailed over my shoulders and down my arms. Her lips traced soft kisses down my neck making me moan.

"I am afraid I will miss this," I confessed, leaning farther back into her.

"It isn't over yet," she replied. "Just enjoy the time we have."

I sighed and relaxed into her touch.

We stayed in the bath until the water cooled and gooseflesh started to creep across my skin.

"I have an errand to run," Grace said as she rung water out of her hair. "But I won't be long."

She reached for her clothes.

"Oh no, captain." I locked my hands behind her neck and drew her in, stopping before our lips touched. "You really think you can just walk away from me now that we have our proper bed?"

Grace groaned. "Why is it impossible to say no to you?"

I leaned in to catch her bottom lip in my teeth. "Because you are still mine, Grace."

She hummed in agreement as I kissed her.

"On the bed," I commanded, breaking away from her. "Right now."

Her eyebrows rose and she smirked as she waggled them. "Yes, ma'am."

She swayed her hips as she climbed onto the mattress, looking back at me over her shoulder. "How do you want me?"

I had had something else in mind, but the sight of her nude, still damp from our bath and eager for me, made it all fly away with the need to simply pleasure the incredible woman in front of me.

I climbed onto the bed beside her and lay flat on my back.

"Come here." My voice was hoarse with arousal.

She made to straddle my hips, but I grabbed her thighs and shimmied farther down while pulling her up so that her knees were either side of my head. I had never done this before, but I had read about it in a book of salacious stories I found in Madame's studio whilst she had been otherwise occupied. I had been too shy to ask to try it at the time, but the idea had stuck with me, sometimes sneaking into my mind when I was alone in my bed.

"Sit," I commanded, giving her backside a hard swat to encourage her. "Hold onto the headboard and sit."

Grace did so hesitantly and too slowly for my liking. I was impatient and needed to taste her. I grabbed her hips and forced her down onto my mouth.

There was no teasing this time. No careful little licks and sucks. No playfulness.

I simply devoured her.

She shrieked as she found her release, and the bed shook as her legs spasmed around my head. I let her roll off me. Her heaving breasts shone with perspiration, and I could not stop myself from taking one in my mouth, smearing her skin in the evidence of her pleasure that dripped from my chin.

"Oh, I will absolutely need you to do that again before you leave," Grace panted. She had thrown her forearm over her eyes. I loved that as many times as we had gone to bed together, shyness still overcame her afterwards.

"With pleasure," I murmured as I took her nipple between my teeth.

She shook her head. "No time. I have things that must be done today. I will return with a gift for you, but I must leave now."

"So good to me," I mumbled as I trailed kisses down her stomach.

She caught my face and drew me back up to crash her lips into mine. Lord, this woman was a good kisser. Her tongue flicked against mine. I got so lost in it I had not realized she had flipped us over until she drew away and I was once again on my back.

"Be good and stay here. I will return soon."

"Can I come with you?"

"It's better if you are not seen. You stand out, love. I do not want to risk your father's men coming for you before the meeting." She winked at me as she retrieved the last of her clothing. "I still want paid."

"Pirate," I muttered.

"Indeed." She stooped to give me one last chaste kiss. "So be a good little hostage and stay here. Don't make me tie you to the bed."

I grinned at her and stretched out so that my fingertips grazed the headboard.

"Are you threatening me with a good time, captain?"

Grace let out a pained groan.

"You will be the death of me, woman." She set her hat on her tousled hair. "Lock the door behind me. I'll be back soon."

Chapter Twenty Two

I did not mean for sleep to take me so readily but I was awoken sometime later by the soft scraping of the key in the lock as my captain returned. I rubbed my eyes as I sat up.

"You have returned already?"

"I've been gone for hours." She scanned my rumpled hair and the lines the sheets had left on my face. "Enjoy your nap?"

"Mhm." I stretched lazily. "Best sleep I have had in a long time."

"Get up," she commanded in the same tone she once used to rouse me for a day's work.

"Yes, captain," I replied cheekily and rose, letting the sheets fall away until I stood before her completely nude.

Grace's eyes traced every one of my curves. Her dark eyes flickered as she licked her lower lip. I never tired of the reaction my body elicited from her. She had confessed late one night how hard she had to try to keep her attraction to me hidden. The night I saw her pleasure herself in her bunk was far from the only time she had indulged to the thought of me.

"I was going to get you to try on your new dress, but…"

"You bought me a dress?"

"I did. I have to have you looking your best if I'm to get the best price for you." She sucked in a breath as her eyes trailed my body. "It would be hard to improve on this though."

I arched an eyebrow and tilted my chin in challenge. "Are you simply going to look?"

"Absolutely not."

The way she stalked towards me made me tingle. I loved that predatory side of her. I was tempted to run away from her just so that she would chase me. She must have guessed what I was thinking because she lunged forwards before I could make a move and threw me, squealing, onto the bed.

She was on me in a second, pinning my wrists down to the sheets. Her mouth crashed into mine in a scorching kiss. I gasped into it as her knee wedged itself between my thighs.

"You know what that does to me," I groaned, arching underneath her and chasing the delicious friction of her leg between mine.

Her mouth was hot and wet as it teased my nipples. She was relentless and I writhed under her.

"If you want me to fuck you, love, then you'll have to beg for it."

I groaned again. One of her hands released my wrist and wrapped firmly around my throat as her hips rolled against me.

"Just one little word and I'll give you what you want."

"Please," I whispered, clawing at the sheets under me. "Please, please, plea—"

She thrust into me before I was even done begging her to.

"You are so wet," she growled, hiking one of my legs up over her shoulder as she sat back on her knees, two fingers buried inside of me. She set a punishing pace.

"Grace!"

"I love it when you scream for me."

My leg was stretched up, spreading me wide open as she leaned in to kiss me. She kept her mouth on mine as she added a third finger, swallowing my moans of pleasure. Her fist was tight in my hair as she kissed me like her life depended on it. The sting in my scalp, the aching stretch of her fingers. Pain mixed with pleasure so intense I thought I might lose my mind from it. Heat uncoiled deep in my belly, making me arch my back and tip my head back in a silent scream as my orgasm racked through me and Grace coaxed every ounce of gratification out of me.

The next few hours were a heady, intoxicating blur. The captain's clothing was strewn across the floor. The only thing she wore was her tricorne. I had asked her to keep it on as I granted her request for a repeat of our earlier activities, amongst other things. I closed my eyes—happy, warm and content nestled in the sheets. I had never felt so thoroughly satisfied before and sleep was tugging at the edges of my mind again.

Back on the Bone Heart, Grace and I had often talked after we made love whilst caressing each other or simply holding one another tight. We spoke of the stars, of art and of lost stories. We spoke of past lovers, future wishes, hopes and fears. She told me amusing anecdotes about members of the crew and I shared tales from home.

Tonight, however, I knew that if we spoke, then we would speak of my leaving. I did not wish to think of that, not while I still had Grace naked in my arms. I wished to treasure this last night together. Sadness was coming for us both but that did not mean we had to hasten its arrival and so I stayed silent. Grace did too.

I had thought that she was also as worn out as I until she left my embrace to crawl down the bed. I jerked up when I felt her between my legs, but she grasped my thighs and pulled me back to her mouth.

"I am nowhere near done with you," she said. Her voice muffled but there was an urgency too it. She too was avoiding the truth of what the following day would bring.

"You are going to haunt me, Grace," I groaned as her tongue brushed over my swollen and sensitive clit. "Tell me you will not forget me when you are at sea."

"How could I? How could I ever forget your taste? The way you feel? The way you make me feel"?"

Her teeth grazed my skin, making me moan. I pressed my hand over my mouth, but she pulled it away.

"No, love. We're not on the ship anymore. You do not have to be quiet." She bit me hard as her fingers plunged into me once again and I let out a cry. "I want this whole damn port to hear when I make you scream."

Chapter Twenty Three

"One round and then we go," the captain announced sternly as she ordered the rum. I found myself more nervous than I expected and was all too glad of the spiced liquor as I joined the crew members that Grace had recruited to come with us.

"A little intimidation is always good for coaxing tight purse strings," Grace had told me when I questioned the need for all the muscle joining us.

We were meeting a contact of my father's just outside of the town at sundown. He would pay Captain Halliwell the agreed ransom, and I would go with him to board a ship back to Beauris. It was simple arrangement.

I should have been happy. I was finally going home. No more pirates, no more violence, no more hard labor...no more Grace. I almost told her to call it off as we left the inn, but I bit my tongue. I had to go back to my real life.

Although the inn boasted a large stable, it appeared that we were to walk to our destination. That surprised me since the captain had to claim a bad case of sea-legs as she wobbled into the dining room earlier. I smirked at her boldfaced lie, knowing full well that my tongue was the cause.

My own knees trembled just as much but my dress hid that fact beneath the soft fabric. I was wearing the new blue dress that the captain had purchased for me. On the surface, it was nothing special—a simple but well-made garment—but I would have chosen it over my finest gowns.

My displeasure at the thought of walking waned with

the fluttering of brightly colored birds overhead and the rich, scent of sweet flowers that crawled up the sides of the buildings.

Grace murmured as she walked beside me, "I thought you should at least see some more sights before you go home. Years ago, traders brought exotic plants and animals here from the southern seas and a good part of it thrived. It is a hidden oasis in northern seas."

"It is beautiful. Do you come here often?"

Grace shrugged. "Now and again. It is beautiful but not high on my list for trade. But if you want information from the mainland, then this is as good a spot as any."

I chewed my lip as we passed various drinking establishments that were filling up and smaller shops that were closing for the night. I would never get a chance to explore them. I would never get a chance to explore a lot of things once I was back in the comforts of my family home. Each step towards the meeting point was a leaden weight in my stomach. I would be fine once I was truly home, I told myself. These were all small regrets in the grand scheme of things. In a year, they would not matter to me anymore. *She* would not matter to me.

If only I believed the lies I told myself.

The farther we walked, the wider the space between dwellings and the fewer people meandered past. I caught a few furtive glances that came our way, but no one bothered us. It might have been the armory that hung from the hips of my companions. Grace had insisted I take a small knife too. As idyllic as Cineria appeared to be, in Grace's words, "nowhere is as safe as it looks. Especially for a sweet thing as delectable as you." I smiled at the memory of the kiss that followed the statement.

The town had fallen away behind us, and the long shadows cast from the torches that the men held made me shiver despite the mildness of the evening. My desire to call the whole thing off was once again on the tip of my tongue. Instead, I asked the question I had been avoiding since we first set course for Cineria and my journey turned homeward. I knew the answer would knock some sense into me as much as it might break my heart.

"Will I see you again?"

Grace did not look at me. Her face was shadowed by her tricorne hat that she had pulled down low. I could only see her mouth, pulled into a taut grimace.

"If luck is on your side, you'll never get tangled up with pirates again, sweetpea."

"That is not what I asked."

Grace sighed.

"I will not be stopping by for tea if that is what you're asking."

I nodded, not trusting myself to speak around the lump that had formed in my throat. Of course, she would not. I knew that. I expected it. So why did I feel like my heart was being carved out?

I jumped in surprise as her hand slid into mine. She squeezed once and her lips curved in a smile.

"But should you ever find yourself wanting to run away again, you would find a welcome place on my ship."

I cleared my throat. I managed to return her smile. I would be just as likely to repeat my seafaring adventures as she was to come to tea and we both knew it. This was farewell.

The night was quiet apart from the sounds of birds and our own footsteps so when a twig snapped up ahead, we all froze.

"Eyes open, lads," the captain growled, drawing her pistol. "It seems we have company. No one would be this far out from the town without a reason."

The sound of weapons being drawn came from all around, not just from the crew behind us but from the shadows ahead.

"Show yourself!" Grace barked.

I flinched and yanked my own little knife out of its holder. My hands shook but I held it tightly. I did not survive all this to get murdered by bandits on the road when I was so close to going home.

"Now, now," a voice called from the darkness. It was chiding and almost sounded amused. It made the hair on the back of my neck prickle. "We can deal with this like gentlemen."

"Come out with your hands up!" Grace yelled, pointing her pistol. Her free hand drew her sword.

A man stepped out into the light of the torches, his hands slightly raised. He tutted again. He certainly looked the part of a gentleman from his neatly combed hair right down to his polished dress shoes. His suit was tailored and pressed. His face was familiar... Confusion clouded my mind. Surely not?

"Mr. Thompson?" I whispered. "What are you doing here?"

"Thompson? Your fiancé?" Grace hissed at me.

I nodded.

"Miss Barnett." He nodded to me politely. "Captain Halliwell."

I had not expected Mr. Thompson to be the one to retrieve me, but he was truly here. I supposed he did work with my father and had business in shipping that could have taken him in this direction. It was not unfeasible, just unexpected. Perhaps this was seen as the honorable thing to do? To rescue ones intended?

I took a step towards him, to greet him properly as a lady would a gentleman, but something made me hesitate. No one had lowered their weapons and the air was still thick with tension. What did they see that I could not?

"Grace?" I whispered, tugging on her sleeve. "What is going on?"

"He didn't say the code word. I don't care if you

know him, you are not going with this man. This is not the meeting that I set up."

If I had not been looking straight at Mr. Thompson, I would have missed the slight twitch of his eye at the mention of a codeword. I swallowed hard. Anxiousness plucked at the back of my neck.

"If I tell you to run, do not hesitate. Understand?" Grace muttered out of the corner of her mouth.

"Really, captain. Is that any way to start negotiations? Do you not wish for clean deal?" Mr. Thompson asked, impatience creeping into his voice.

"There is nothing to negotiate. She's not going with you."

He smiled and waved a hand dismissively. "She will be coming with us, but those are not the negotiations of which I speak. I've heard you came across some interesting maps recently. I would like to be taking those with me as well. They will be very good for business."

My stomach dropped. Grace's knuckles were white as she gripped her sword. The foliage behind Mr. Thompson rustled.

"Enough of this. Elise, *run*. Men advance!"

The crew that had accompanied us surged forward.

Ramsden drew his pistol.

"Drop your weapons!" He turned and pressed it against Grace's head. "*Captain*."

Chapter Twenty Four

"What the hell are you doing, Ramsden?" Grace snarled.

"Drop. Your. Weapons."

I tore my gaze from Grace as a pistol was levelled at me too. Raul at least had the decency to give me an apologetic shrug as he nodded to my weapon. Even if he played beautiful music, he was as much a pirate as the rest of them. I doubted he would regret my death. In any case, staring down the barrel, my little knife seemed pitiful in comparison. I dropped it.

Grace's eyes darted to me. It was a startling realization that the fear I saw there was not for her own life but for mine. If she had been on her own, if I had not been a factor, she may have chosen differently. She glanced to Ramsden and then up to the pistol that was still pressing into her skull. Her eyes stayed locked on mine as she let her own pistol fall from her hand. Her sword followed.

As soon as her weapons hit the sandy ground, Ramsden's fist met her jaw. Grace stumbled, falling to one knee.

"No!" I screamed. "Do not hurt her!"

Someone grabbed my arms from behind as I tried to run to her.

Grace tried to rise, but Ramsden's pistol was back, pressed hard against her head and keeping her on the ground as Ramsden kicked her sword into the foliage and out of her reach. She spat blood.

I had thought sailing away and never seeing her again

was going to be the hardest thing I had ever done, but it did not come even close to seeing her in pain. In that moment I saw things more clearly that I ever had in my life. I could not leave her. I could not leave to go back to a life of hiding who I was and what I felt. I could not leave us behind. Her fire, her wit, her smile, her gentle soul that she hid behind spiked walls. She was all that I wanted. I needed her like I needed air. And she needed me too. I saw it written in the pain and regret splashed across her face as she glanced up at me again.

"Run," she mouthed, her lips stained red with her own blood.

"Not without you," I panted as I struggled to free myself.

I twisted my face round to demand whoever was holding me release me immediately so that I could go to her. When I saw his face, however, my stomach flipped. I knew that face too. Gerald, with his pale blue eyes, neat moustache and spotless suit. Madame's manservant. And if he was here…

"Well, well, well. I did not think we would ever meet again, Grace."

Grace's face was a blank mask of shock at the voice.

"Madame Chevalier?" I whispered as the woman stepped out of the shadows. "How are you here? What is going on?!"

"Chevalier?" Grace blinked hard. "No, her name is Carter. Rosemary Carter."

"Rosemary? As in your lover", Rosemary?" My own mouth gaped open. "You were Grace's lover?"

Madame gave me the same pitying look she would give me whenever I struggled to grasp new techniques. "My dear pearl, hush now. You need not concern yourself with the past."

"You were her lover all those years ago," I whispered and then frowned. "Are you not glad to see her alive? She said you never knew what happened."

Madame smiled.

"Oh, she knew," Grace snarled, realization giving way to fury. "Didn't you? You were behind it. You wanted me dead all those years. I remember now. That was the night I told you I wouldn't run away with you. She called me her pearl, too."

I could not have said what I was feeling in that moment. Shock, confusion, hurt and fear all swirled and collided in my chest. I should have been more concerned that armed pirates were surrounding me but the only thing that pierced the fog of my tumultuous emotions was one thing. Madame called someone else her pearl.

"Is that true?" I gasped.

Madame gave Grace an impassionate look as she turned to me.

"I came to collect you, my pearl. Dear Mr Thompson was happy to assist when he knew you had been taken by the famous Bone Heart. Whispers of their little treasure hunt has been making the rounds for many months now." The smile she gave me sent chills through my bones.

No one was supposed to know about the treasure. Grace had trusted him, and Ramsden had been plotting against her from the beginning. The pieces of the puzzle slid together.

"You bastard," Grace hissed up at Ramsden through her teeth. "All this time?"

He sneered down at her. "Since the day you stabbed old Lucky in the heart. He should have been captain. Not you. You're only alive because of the old captain's superstitions. He should have left you in the harbor where he found you."

"I'm going to make you wish I died that day when I'm through with you."

Even on her knees, bleeding and surrounded, Grace still managed to be intimidating and I noticed Ramsden suppress a flinch.

"It has been, let's see…eleven years since then?" Madame Chevalier seemed unaffected by the tension. She spoke as if she were discussing the weather. "I must say, I did not think I would be seeing you again, Grace."

"Did you know you were putting Elise on my ship? Of course, you did. I bet you got some sick pleasure out of that. You wanted me to do your dirty work for you. You wanted me to get rid of her like your man should have gotten rid of me." Grace's voice had risen to a shout.

Her expression hardened and, even with blood still dripping down her front, she bared her bloody teeth and launched herself at Madame Chevalier. She did not get far. The butt of a rifle was slammed into her back. She hit the ground hard. Ramsden planted his boot on her head and ground her face into the dirt.

I was unsure when I started screaming but I was. I was fighting and screaming for all I was worth for them to leave her alone. For them not to hurt her. I would throw myself in front of her and defend her until my last breath if I could only reach her. Gerald's grip on my arms tightened as I struggled.

"Will you take her away?" Madame snapped, frowning at me like I was nothing more than an annoyance. "Put her in my carriage."

"No!" I shouted at the same time Grace bellowed for them not to touch me.

I would not be able to help her. Terror clouded my mind. If I were taken away now, I may never see Grace alive again. I was hoisted and thrown over a hard shoulder and no amount of kicking seemed to deter Gerald from his task.

Over my own screams, I heard Mr. Thompson's hard voice.

"Where are the maps, Ms. Halliwell? We can do this the easy way or the hard way."

She would never give up those maps. The true

treasure, she had called them. She had sweated and bled for them, and my hard-headed, stubborn pirate captain would let them torture her all night without saying a word.

Gerald turned and, without a word, began to carry me away. Twisting, I could still see Grace on the ground. She was surrounded. Her former crew and Mr. Thompson's men. Ramsden removed his boot from her head and let her haul herself to her knees. He kept her there with the point of his sword resting at her throat. I could not hear her words anymore as I was carried farther away, but I saw Grace grin and spit in his face. He cracked the pommel of his sword against her temple. She crumpled.

I screamed again but she lay still. No, no, no! Panic rose like bile in my throat, but I forced myself to think. They needed her secrets. She could not be dead. They would not kill her, no, not yet. Not until they knew where the maps were. They were going to hurt her, though. They were going to hurt her, and I could do nothing to stop it. I could not bear the thought and I fought for all I was worth.

"Let me go!" I raged against Gerald's grip as he turned a corner, and I lost sight of the group altogether. "Please! Let me go to her!"

I was jostled and I thought at first that it was deliberate to increase my discomfort and silence me, but then I realized he was laughing.

"You may as well settle down. They won't kill her yet, but Grace Halliwell will be dead soon enough. The king's men pay a pretty penny for pirates."

Gerald did not carry me for very long and, even though the blood rushed from my head when I was set down, I immediately tried to run back to her. I did not even manage one step before his arm wrapped around my waist.

"In," he growled.

Only then did I realize he had set me down in front of a carriage. The driver sat stiff-backed and facing forward.

He had probably been promised a chunk of gold for his silence. I would find no help there.

Gerald shoved me inside the carriage and into the seat. I wrenched at the opposite door handle, but it did not budge.

"Where are you taking me?" I asked, my breaths coming in hard and fast.

He ignored me.

"Let me out!" I yanked at the door handle again.

The door opened barely seconds later to reveal Madame Chevalier. As poised and graceful as ever, she settled herself across from me but a line appeared between her eyebrows as she frowned. She reached out and tried to tuck a wayward strand of hair behind my ear, but I jerked away from her touch. I barely stopped myself from dragging my nails down her face just like I had when I thought Grace was a monster.

"Do not touch me," I hissed.

"You used to enjoy my touch. Very much if I recall correctly."

Once upon a time, I used to love that self-assured smile. I ignored the heat that rose to my face.

"Where is Grace? What have you done with her?" I demanded. "I swear—"

"Grace?" Her eyebrow rose and a different kind of smile played across her face. As if she knew with just that word how much she meant to me. "I must say, I did not anticipate you two becoming fond of each other. You can put Ms. Halliwell out of your mind, now."

"Tell me!"

"Do not raise your voice to me," she said sternly but then relaxed. "My men will bring her along. I shall hand her over to the king's guard as soon as she talks, and then I imagine she will be executed before long."

My blood ran cold.

"How could you? How can you not care? I know who she was to you."

Madame's smile turned nasty.

"What she was to me was a distraction. A small delay in pursuit of better things. Besides, she was destined to die years ago. Things are finally being put right."

"And me? You really meant for me to die, did you not?" I meant it to sound accusing, but it came out as barely more than a whisper. My lip was trembling. I had been so scared for Grace that I had only just now realized the danger to myself. "Are you going to kill me?"

Madame laughed. I had once thought her laugh to be like the tinkling of bells but that another piece of the part she had played. This laugh was a harsh bark devoid of merriment. I flinched.

"No, no. I plan on collecting that filthy pirate's ransom for you. To kill you before I get it would just be a waste of easy money."

I swallowed.

"And after?"

"We shall see."

"And Mr. Thompson? What is his role in this?"

"A means to an end. His company have been chasing after that ludicrous sunken treasure for years now. Our alliance was simply too good of an opportunity to set aside." Madame lifted a shoulder as if to say the matter was concluded. "I believe it is now Mr. Thompson's intention to withdraw his proposal and take to the seas with dear Grace's maps. He will have no need of a dowry if they are as lucrative as he describes. That money will come to me as your ransom. As pretty a thing as you are, you are not as appealing a prospect as you once were with not a penny to your name."

I tried not to be offended. I had far greater problems to deal with, but it still stung that my worth was so easily written off. If this all came down to money, perhaps there was still room to negotiate.

"Let me go. Let us both go, and I will give you the money as payment for our lives," I pleaded. "Please, do not hurt her!"

Again, that horrible laugh.

"And just how would you save your captain when the king's guard has already heard word that she has been sighted on this island, hm? More likely, you would be shot on sight attempting to flee. Also, that would require trusting the two of you to honor your word. After today, I find it difficult to believe that dear Grace would be so forgiving."

"You could trust me."

She leant forward. "Trust is what got you into this mess. I do not make those mistakes and I cannot have you blabbing to anyone about me. I have a reputation to uphold. Now, I do not want to hear any more of it."

She was back to my stern tutor.

"If you let me go now, I will not tell anyone what you have done. I promise. Neither of us will say a word!"

"Enough."

"Please!"

The look she gave me had me shrinking back into my seat. For a second, I was sure she would strike me, but she simply folded her hands in her lap and stared me down.

But I refused to cower. Not anymore. I lifted my chin.

"How many have there been? How many young women have you played with, robbed and made disappear? How many *pearls*?"

She sighed and when she smoothed my hair back, I did not move away. "You know, I never thought to count."

This time, I did go for her face. I did not quite manage to scratch her as I had intended, but I did poke her in the eye before her manservant got his hands on me and wrestled my arms behind my back. I screamed and kicked until he had me pressed against the side of the carriage and I could barely move.

Two loud taps sounded through the interior from the coachman rapping on the roof. My outburst had sent the whole carriage rocking, and even now that I was held still, the carriage swayed alarmingly.

"Really, Elise!"

My mind was aflame. I could not get out. I could not move. Grace was going to die. Madame called me Elise. She never called me Elise. I was her pearl. Her sweet girl. Never Elise. Grace…

It all hit me at once. Grace had been right. I really was nothing to her. I had been naïve, foolish, stupid with love for a woman who had never earned it. She had gotten what she wanted from me and now…now…

My heart stuttered. She really was going to kill me.

I sat in stunned silence, letting the realization wash over me as Madame's manservant tied my hands behind my back.

"Where are you taking me?" I finally asked.

"I have many properties across the islands. We are going to one where we will not be disturbed," Madame answered, still dabbing at her eye with a silk handkerchief. "Your father's courier…was delayed shall we say? He will not arrive with the ransom for a few days still."

I swallowed hard. I still had a few days to live.

Chapter Twenty Five

"It is not too late to let me go," I tried again to reason with Madame as the carriage drew to a halt. "You do not have to do this."

"Enough, Elise, we have been over this."

Again, it stung for her to use my name. It just proved that she was finished with me. I was going to plead further but, at that point, her manservant opened the door next to me and dragged me out. I had always the impression of him being a frail, older man, but he handled me with ease as I tried with all my strength to pull away.

"Walk or I shall carry you," he said, yanking on my arm.

I shot him a glare but stopped resisting as he towed me towards a villa with white walls and a tiled roof. Columns lined the porch and leafy plants spilled out of huge vases on either side of the door I was marched through.

The interior was airy, and our footsteps clacked on the tile underfoot. I was unsurprised by the tasteful décor and evident luxury of the marble entryway, but what took my breath away was the stack of canvases leaning against the far wall. I stumbled to a halt. I knew those paintings as intimately as I knew myself. As I looked up at the art that decorated the walls, I realized that I knew every painting in this room.

"Are those...Are those mine?" I whispered as fragments of my own soul looked back at me from within their wall-mounted frames. "My paintings?"

"Indeed," Madame replied, trailing a fingertip over

one of the gilded frames. It was one I had painted of her at her studio—an elegant portrait with just a hint of skin showing where her silken robe parted. It had been one of my favorites. "They sell surprisingly well. Of course, the price will only increase when news of the artist's death hits the markets. You shall be making me money for a long time, my dear."

It registered in the back of my mind that I should be afraid that she had all but confirmed her plan to do away with me once she had the money, but my fear was nothing compared to the anger that reared its head.

"Have you not taken enough from me?!" I spat.

"I shall keep some of them, of course. I never lied about your talent, my pearl."

"How dare you call me that?" Gerald had to grasp both my arms to stop me throwing myself at her again. "How dare you!"

"I see your time in dear Grace's company has done your manners no favors at all," Madame sighed as if I had disappointed her and then nodded to her manservant, who hoisted me over his shoulder once again.

"Put me down!" I protested to no avail as he carried me farther inside.

My view changed from the entranceway tiles to stairs and then carpet. I heard only Gerald's heavy footsteps, meaning that Madame had left me yet again.

He finally set me down on a bed in a sparse room. Madame's taste for luxury had not extended to every corner of her property it seemed. Perhaps this was meant to be servants' quarters. The slats of the bed creaked with my weight as I tried to sit up. With my arms still bound behind me, it was not the most graceful of motions, but I managed it. Madame's manservant stood beside the bed, untangling a new length of cord. Perhaps I could reason with him or, at the very least, distract him before I was truly helpless.

"Gerald, please. Can you not see this is wrong?

Whatever she is paying you, I shall double it if you help me."

He snorted. "She doesn't pay me. She is my wife."

"Your...wife," I echoed in disbelief.

She was married. All this time, she had a husband. And he was in her house...he had greeted me every time I visited. He had poured me tea and smirked because he knew what we had been doing. He was her husband.

My stomach flipped at another realization.

Grace had told me it was her lover's husband that had attacked her. Stabbed her and left her for dead. *Gerald* had tried to kill her.

I could hardly believe that the mild-mannered gentleman servant could have done such a thing. Then again, he had just helped kidnap me. How could I have seen none of this coming? Madame had played me for a fool.

"How can she be your wife?" I whispered.

"You mean how can I allow my wife to bed her young student?" His thin lips quirked up in a smile that made the skin on the back of my neck prickle.

My face flushed. Before I could answer, he had pushed me back down on the mattress. I tried my hardest to escape his touch. Lord only knew how much blood had coated those hands from how many innocent fools like me. I grunted as he grasped my ankles and wound the cord around them, cinching it tightly.

"You know, you were one of my favorites to watch. I especially liked the sounds you would make. It's almost a shame we have to keep you quiet now."

Before I could voice my disgust and outrage, he had thrust a strip of fabric in between my lips.

"I thought she should have kept you as her pearl for a little while longer. You had not yet gotten tedious," he said conversationally while knotting the strip behind my head. "But it never takes her long to find a new one."

If my mouth had been free, I would have uttered

curses that would have made my mother faint.

"Your pirate captain was one of her first." His eyes glittered as he smoothed my hair back, checking that none of it was caught in the gag. "But she was the first that refused to disappear. My darling wife has been keeping an eye on her for years, waiting for this chance. In a way, you made this happen. I'm sure she is very grateful. I know I am."

He brought his mouth so close to my ear that his breath tickled my cheek.

"I think I shall go into town when they execute her. I do so like to watch."

Chapter Twenty Six

I do not know how long I lay on that bed after Madame's husband left, locking the door behind him. Her husband. How could I have been so blind? I fought my bindings until I was breathless, but there was no slack to be found and all I achieved was stinging chafes. The house around me was far from silent— I could hear the comings and goings of footsteps and the general bustle of a household. If anyone could hear them no one responded to my muffled screams for help. Lord, my throat was so dry. My attempts to dislodge the cloth were also in vain and it remained stubbornly in place.

I refused to let myself cry. Whatever my discomfort, it was nothing to what was probably happening to Grace at that moment. I felt sick to my stomach when I thought of what they could be doing to her, of the pain she could be in. I had to get out of here and soon. Not just to save my own life, but hers too. I just had to hope that she held out until I could get to her. We would find a way out of this together.

I tried once again to free myself, tugging and writhing, ignoring the pain in my wrists. The room I was trapped in was bare. Nothing but the bed I lay on and a washstand. If I could get off the bed, I decided, I could perhaps find some rough edge to cut the cords. Rolling off the bed was a momentous task in itself, but it appeared I had all the time in the world to achieve it. I braced myself for the impact as I finally maneuvered the bulk of my weight to the edge and tipped over but it still winded me. I would definitely have bruises on my shoulder and hip to deal with if I lived through my escape attempt.

I wormed my way to the foot of the bed and felt around for any splinters or wayward nails that I could use to cut myself loose. My questing fingers were rewarded by a sharp jab, and I rejoiced in the pain and wetness of blood I felt on my fingertip. It was time to get to work.

It was a war of wills between my stubborn determination and that of the cords. So far, they were winning. I was exhausted, slick with sweat, and I kept tumbling over onto my side and having to relocate the sharp nail that was to be my savior. I was sure each and every one of my fingers had been pricked by it as I fumbled to find it again and cried out silently.

I resigned myself to taking a rest and lay with my heated cheek pressed to the cool, wooden floor. I desperately needed some water.

Because my face was against the floor, I felt the frantic footsteps before I heard them. A pounding that was coming closer until someone rattled the handle of my door. It was locked, of course. I tried to call out. It ended up closer to a pitiful, mewling sound but whoever it was heard me.

"Someone there?" A quiet, gruff voice whispered through the keyhole.

I knew that voice. Tears leaked from the corners of my eyes, and I screamed for all I was worth to let Petra know that she had found me. A quiet curse from outside was followed by a metallic scraping sound as the lock was picked.

"Good gods, girl. What've you gotten yourself into?"

Knees thumped down beside my head. I was lifted up into a sitting position. Petra's stern, wrinkled face appeared before mine as she yanked away the fabric that kept me quiet.

"Pet—" My voice broke, and I coughed.

"Shush now. Let's get you out of here. Here." She held a hipflask to my lips. It may not have been the water I had been so desperate for, but the rum did at least bring a little moisture to my tongue.

Someone else knelt at my back and made quick work of my bonds. I groaned in relief as they fell away and I could roll my shoulders. My hands were a bloodied mess.

"Looks like you almost didn't need us." Sully waggled his eyebrows at me. "You were almost through the rope."

"Good to see you haven't just been lazing around."

I scowled at the old cook, ready to tell her exactly what I had been through when I saw her eyes were crinkled up in a smile. I smiled back.

"Thank you," I said earnestly. "For coming for me."

"Part of the crew, ain't ya?" Petra replied roughly, accepting the knife from Sully to cut through the ties at my ankles.

"The crew that betrayed us, you mean?"

Petra's lip curled back in a snarl. "They're no crew of mine. Where is the captain?"

My stomach flipped. I hoped to God that we were not too late.

"She is here somewhere. I do not know where. They were going to torture her for the location of the maps. We have to hurry!"

Petra grasped my forearm and hauled me to my feet.

"How did you find us?" I asked in a whisper as we tiptoed along the corridor.

Petra snorted. "Those disloyal bastards were bragging. Said they got easy gold for giving you up. There ain't a lot of folks who can afford the kind of coin, and it only took a few careful questions to find this place."

"You were not tempted to side with them? I can imagine how much gold they received for both of us." I looked between them. Petra I could understand. She had always seemed the closest to Grace but Sully had been friendly with

Marcos and Ramsden. I narrowed my eyes at the boy.

"Petra threatened to string me up from the mast if I didn't help." Sully grinned.

"The cap'n has my loyalty. I'd take her over any of those dogs no matter the coin," Petra growled back. "I've known Gracie a long time, and I know that if she hadn't been taken as well, she'd have burnt heaven and earth to come after you."

That made me smile. The image of Grace, sword in hand, battling the world for me. In my heart, I knew it was true too because I would do the same for her. I would take this villa apart brick by brick if I had to and, once I had her back in my arms I was never, ever letting go.

"We have to find her," I said, determination furrowing my brow.

"Aye. Keep an eye out while we check these last few rooms."

The house was empty and eerie. The servants that I had heard bustling about must have retired hours ago. I shuffled to the window and peeked out. If I were holding a dangerous pirate prisoner, then I would have patrols circling the building especially before the sun had risen. It seemed Madame agreed, and the glow of torches passed by below as the guards made their rounds. Hopefully that meant there were no guards inside and we could find Grace without interference.

I was about to indicate to Petra that the coast was clear when one of the doors between us swung open. Petra ducked into a doorway, but I was trapped in the middle of the corridor with nowhere to hide.

"Why you little..."

Gerald's eyes narrowed as he spotted me. He must have been coming to check on me. He set the water jug he carried on a side table as he drew a knife from the inside of his jacket.

"You are starting to be more trouble than you are worth," he snarled. No trace of his gentlemanly countenance remained as he stalked towards me.

I backed into the window ledge, cornered, desperately looking for anything that I could use as a weapon, but there was nothing. The look on his face told me he was not planning on just taking me back to my room but making me thoroughly regret escaping it in the first place.

"I shall just have to—"

His eyes went wide, his mouth slack, as the tip of Petra's sword burst through his chest. I covered my mouth to suppress my scream and the world stood still for a moment before Petra's sword slid free with a sickly wet sound.

Gerald was dead before he hit the floor. Bile started to climb up my throat as his blank eyes stared through me. His lifeless face was sure to haunt my dreams if I lived through the night.

"Good riddance." Petra spat on his corpse and then turned to me. "Grace isn't up here. This place must have a cellar so you—"

"Gerry!"

The scream came from the top of the staircase. Both Petra and I turned as Madame Chevalier rushed forth and fell to her knees next to Gerald's body.

I did not hesitate.

I seized the water jug that Gerald had left on the side table and swung it with all my strength, bringing it down on Madame Chevalier's head. The shattered crystal fell with her, creating a merry tinkling sound as it rained down on the hard floor.

I stared open-mouthed at the crumpled form of my former tutor. She did not move as blood started to seep into the carpet.

Petra looked me up and down appraisingly. "Not bad, stowaway."

"Is she dead?" I whispered.

Petra nudged Madame's fallen form with her foot.

"I'd say so, aye. Now move!" She shoved me towards the stairs.

"Oh lord, I killed her," I whispered as we crept downwards. I felt numb. I had killed someone. No, not just someone. I killed Madame Chevalier. My stomach lurched. I pressed my hand over my mouth and groaned. I could not afford to be sick right now.

"Shut up. Guards are crawling all over the place on the lower levels so keep sharp," Petra hissed. "I'll go find Sully and keep them occupied."

"What should I do?" I cried, wringing my hands.

She looked at me as if I had just asked her if water was wet.

"First, pull yourself together, you fool," she growled and smacked me on the side of the head. "Then go save your captain."

Chapter Twenty Seven

I had not seen Petra take the keys from Gerald's body, but she had along with his knife, both of which she pressed into my hands and bid me luck. I took a deep breath. She was right. I had to pull myself together. For Grace.

I tiptoed down the stone stairs into the cellar, my heart hammering in my chest. The air was cold here and gooseflesh sprang up along my arms.

"Grace?" I called out in a whisper.

My own voice echoed back at me, making me shiver.

I passed empty room after empty room. Panic crawled up my spine. What if she was not here? What if I was too late?

"Grace?" I called again.

A strained groan from one of the last doors answered me. My heart leapt with hope.

I ran the last few steps to a solid wooden door that was locked with a heavy, rusted padlock. I pressed my ear to the surface and knocked, calling out softly, but only my own heartbeat answered me.

I was sure I had heard something. I tried almost every key on the ring with shaking hands and eventually the lock dropped to the floor with a clang.

I opened the door.

It was pitch-black inside, but the light from a high window behind me illuminated the makeshift cell and its occupant.

When the shard of moonlight hit her face, my heart

seized. Her hair was matted with blood and her face a mess of bruised swelling. She was bound as I had been and sprawled face down on the dusty floor like she had been thrown in to the cell and had not had the strength to move from where she landed.

But she was alive.

A sob of relief escaped me as I rushed to her side.

"Sweetpea?" she croaked incredulously. Her lip was a bloodied mess, and fresh blood welled from the cut as she tried to speak.

"Yes, it is me. I am going to get you out," I whispered as I sawed through her bonds with Gerald's knife. The fingers on her left hand were bent and misshapen, and she moaned when I accidentally brushed them. Tears welled up in my eyes as I took in all her injuries, but I forced them away. I would be strong for her. She needed me to be strong.

"I'm dreaming," Grace mumbled and closed her eyes again.

"You are not dreaming. I am here. Petra is upstairs."

"This is real?"

I helped her sit up, and she reached out to me with her uninjured hand. I took it in my own. She let out a shuddering breath and tears rolled down her cheeks.

"You're really here. You came for me."

"Of course I did," I whispered, pressing a kiss to her palm. "Let us get you out of here."

I looped her arm around my neck and helped her get her feet underneath her.

"Where's the bitch?" Grace asked through gritted teeth. I did not need to ask to whom she was referring.

"I hit her with a jug. I doubt she will trouble us anymore."

Grace huffed out a laugh. "Good girl."

From the tight clench of her jaw, she was in a lot of pain, even if she swore that she was fine. She could barely walk, and I could not carry her full weight. By the time Petra met us at the top of the stairs, sweat was dripping from my brow and my knees were buckling.

"Took you long enough," the cook growled. "The guards are going to notice any second that we—"

Shouts rang out from the upper floors.

Petra shoved her sword into my hands and held out her arms.

"Give me Gracie."

I could not help but smile as the older woman picked up my tough, fearless pirate captain like a wayward kitten and draped her across both her shoulders with ease.

"Petra," Grace whined.

"We move. Now."

"Where is Sully?" I had to trot to keep up with her long strides.

"Gone ahead."

Shouts rang from the upper windows. We had been spotted.

"Run!"

I was ill-suited for running and my dress even more so. As we charged from the villa and into the trees, it caught on low branches, and the layers of fabric threatened to trip me with every step. Curse whoever had brought these wild, tangled things to this island! I was breathless in less than a minute, but the constant sounds of the pursuing guards and crackling gunfire kept me moving with every spare shred of energy I had.

Petra clearly knew this island well because soon she darted off the path and we found ourselves in the low, stony ruins of what might have once been a farmhouse. The old stones were almost swallowed up by vines and ferns and were invisible from the path.

Petra lay Grace in the shadow of one of the old walls and hissed at me to get low and be silent. I dropped to my belly in the foliage, scraping my hands and knees in my urgency, hoping that my hammering heart was not loud enough for us to be caught.

We were still close enough to the path to hear as the guards thundered past our hiding place. I did not dare move until Petra did after long minutes of tense silence. Grace, however, lay still. Her eyes were closed, and her head lolled to the side. I crawled to her as Petra raised herself to a crouch to peek over the ruins.

"Grace?" I whispered but the captain did not wake. Panic stabbed through my heart until I saw the gentle rise and fall of her chest. "Will she be alright?"

I held her battered face in my hands, trying to quell my worries. Captain Halliwell was the strongest woman I knew. She would come back from this. She would come back to me. She had to.

"She's a tough one," was all Petra said in response.

"What do we do now?"

"We wait. Sully is finding us a boat, and then we run like hell from this island and never look back."

"Oh, is that all?" I asked faintly. All I wanted to do was lay down in the soft grass and for this all to be over.

While we waited, Petra tore strips from my dress and used them and some sturdy sticks to splint Grace's broken fingers. The captain stirred and groaned but still did not open her eyes. I held her uninjured hand and traced gentle kisses on her damp forehead until she stilled once more. I hoped that, even though she was not conscious, I could bring her some comfort. My heart ached for her.

A quick peek under her shirt suggested that the rest of her was as black and blue as her face. Petra's forehead creased up with worry as she examined her.

"We must get her to a doctor," I said, my voice thick with horror at the thought of the beating she must have endured. Anger sliced through me. I hoped that the men who had done this to her would get what was coming to them.

Petra shook her head. "Any doctor on this island would turn her in with the king's guard sniffing around. We need to get her away from here."

"How long must we wait?"

As if my words had summoned him, Sully arrived not moments later. He must have run the whole way because his sandy hair was slicked with sweat and he doubled over to brace himself against the stony ruins and catch his breath.

"Is she alive?" he asked in horror, taking in the captain sprawled on the ground.

"Aye. Were you followed?" Petra growled, sword in hand and eyes trained on the shadows in the forest.

"Nay, but we have to go now. I found us a boat, but she won't be unattended for long."

Petra glanced back at the unconscious captain. Her stony expression softened.

"It'll kill her to lose the Heart. She worked so hard for that ship."

"Well, this is no Bone Heart, but she'll float." Sully shrugged.

Petra sniffed and squared her shoulders. "Then it'll do."

Chapter Twenty Eight

Grace's head bobbed forlornly as Petra carried her over her shoulder, but still she slept on. I followed, wringing my hands while constantly peering into shadows for signs of our pursuers. Not that I would be of any help at all if we were pursued. I did not know how to use a weapon and I was not strong enough to carry Grace to safety. Our only hope was to reach our destination undetected. My stomach tied itself in knots over each and every sound.

Sully led us through the tangled foliage until our feet met sand and we could see the outline of the port town in the distance. The earthy smells of the trees gave way to the tang of salt.

"Almost there. Look!" Sully pointed ahead of us to where the sea was lapping against the shore and a single fishing boat was sitting lopsided in the shallows.

We hurried forward, eager to be away from this cursed island.

"How can we be sure they will not follow us?" I asked as Petra waded in up to her knees, Grace cradled in her arms. "The crew could come after us too."

Sully jutted his chin, gesturing behind me. I spun in fear, thinking we had been seen but the beach was empty. Then I looked skywards. A black plume of smoke rose into the clouds.

"They're not going anywhere. The Heart's burning," he said with a quick glance at the unconscious captain.

"Never trust a merchant not to cheat you," Petra

growled. "They're worse than any pirate I ever met."

"Why would they burn the ship?" I asked, edging my way into the shallows as Petra heaved Grace into the boat. Her eyelids fluttered and she grunted as she was set down.

"Grace?" I splashed my way to the side of the boat, but she stilled once more.

"I reckon they didn't find what they were looking for. Ramsden promised them too much. I'd put coin on him burning with it." Petra scowled. "Cast off already, Sully!"

Sully shoved the boat out farther, his skinny arms straining against the hull before clambering in next to me and loosening the sail.

"What now?" I asked in a whisper as the island grew smaller and smaller behind us. The boat that Sully had found for us was tiny, but I would have taken a driftwood raft if it meant we got away.

"Find a crew…Start over…Kill those bastards for burning my ship." To my immense relief, Grace had regained consciousness as we cast off. Her speech was labored, and she was clearly hurting all over, but she spoke with a smile. I noticed with a pang of sympathy that she was now missing a tooth. "What do you say…first mate Petra?"

The older woman looked momentarily dumbfounded.

"If anyone…has earned the title, it's you. I was never meant to be captain…so soon and I appear to have made a right mess of it. But…I'd have done a lot worse without you." She reached out her uninjured hand with a wince.

Petra's eyes shone and she gave a stiff nod as she grasped Grace's hand and shook it.

"Of course I'll be your first mate, Gracie."

Grace blinked at our little boat. "As much as I love…this charming vessel, we need a ship. I have one in mind."

"Are we stealing it?" Sully asked in excitement.

Grace wheezed out a laugh and then clutched her ribs in pain. "You're getting ahead of yourself…We can buy it."

"With what money?" I blurted out.

"The old captain trusted me…with more than just the Bone Heart, love. I never…needed the gold from that wreck."

"You've been sitting on a treasure trove this whole time?!" Sully exclaimed.

"Aye. For emergencies." Grace grimaced as she looked around out stolen vessel. "I'd say this constitutes."

"Can we retrieve it?" I asked getting lost in the excitement of treasure.

"We?" Grace asked in surprise. "You could…go home if you wanted to. I won't stop you."

"Home to what? To be forced into marriage to a man I do not care for?" I stretched luxuriously, tipping my face to the sun. "No, I do not think I shall."

"You want to stay?" The tentative hope in her voice melted my heart. I brushed my lips against hers in the lightest of kisses, wishing I could kiss her as passionately as I wanted to. We would have all the time in the world once she healed.

"I want to stay with you," I said. And I meant it. I would follow my captain to the ends of the earth if it meant staying by her side.

Grace entwined her fingers with mine, her eyes filling with unshed tears and unsaid words, before seemingly remembering we were not alone.

She cleared her throat and nudged me playfully. "Sailed the seas, stole treasure…ran from the king's guards and struck down a sworn enemy. I'd say our sweetpea is…a pretty accomplished pirate."

I blushed at the compliment.

"It's a shame that those bastards will have your maps now, Gracie." Petra glared back in the direction of the island and the smoke rising from the once beloved ship.

"I never…told them a goddamn thing." Grace smiled

wide enough to cause her lip to start bleeding again. "No one will ever get their hands on those maps…I destroyed them." She tapped the side of her head. "It's all up here. That information would've died…with me."

I stroked the side of her face and she leaned into my touch. "You should stop talking and save your energy. We shall find a doctor for you on one of the other islands as soon as we can."

"We'll hunt them down. Ramsden and the rest…the merchant…all of them."

"We will," I promised her. "We will avenge the Bone Heart and make them pay for everything they did to you."

"Together," Grace said firmly.

"Together," I agreed, kissing her temple. "Always."

"I have a name for our new ship already," Grace murmured as her eyes closed. "We shall call her…The Pearl's Revenge."

The End

The Bone Heart

Epilogue

Warmed by the morning sun, soft white sand seeped between my toes as I stepped outside. Despite my initial haste, I still closed my eyes for a second to take a breath of that salty air that still tasted like freedom. The rickety doors of our shack that lead straight onto the beach had been left wide open with the curtains fluttering in the slight ocean breeze.

We had managed for the last few weeks with not a single coin, surviving on the goodwill of old friend of Grace's and a tenuous line of credit on their name. That included the fees for an increasingly anxious doctor. He had treated Grace's injuries with expertise, but I did not trust the way his eyes darted around the room or how he made a point of bringing up payment every chance he could. It was only a matter of time before he or someone else sold us out. It was high time to take our leave and, for that, we needed a ship.

The ship was the reason that Grace did not sleep. She was no longer bruised and battered, and her broken fingers had, although still weak, healed well. Her broken spirit, however, was still in jagged shards. The loss of the Bone Heart had been the greatest injury she had suffered, and it had left a gaping hole in her heart.

I had lain awake and listened to her toss and turn, unsure if I should try to comfort her or not. She had snarled at me more than once not to pity her, and I had often responded with anger of my own. We had not spoken much over the past few days at all, the anxiety of waiting for Petra's return sitting heavy on us both.

All of that changed last night. Petra had returned after finding the treasure exactly where Grace had said it would be as today was the day we were to gain our ship.

I did not have to go far to find Grace when I left the shack that we temporarily called home and stepped out onto the beach. She stood within view, knee-deep in the water, staring out across the horizon. The wind that raced across the waves to ruffle her hair and tug at the loose fabric of her shirt was the only indication that she was not made of stone.

"Grace?" I called as I waded out to meet her.

She did not respond until I was close enough to reach out and touch her.

"I owe you an apology, sweetpea," she said without turning around. Her voice sounded strained. "I owe you so many."

I started to voice my objections when she turned to face me, her expression somber and her eyes damp.

"Don't," she said taking a step towards me. "I have been so awful to you since the day we met. I want you to hear me when I say I am sorry for it."

I swallowed around the lump that had suddenly formed in my throat and nodded.

"I do hear you. And perhaps it should not come to me so readily but I forgive you." I smiled wide. "You shall have plenty of opportunities to make it up to me on our new ship."

She sucked in a sharp breath. "You mean…?"

"Petra has returned. She and Sully sorted payment with the harbor master this morning."

"We got the ship?" Her eyes sparkled with a brightness I had not seen in weeks and the first hints of a smile ghosted across her features.

"We got the ship," I confirmed, my own grin spreading until my cheeks ached. "You are now the captain of the Pearl's Revenge."

With a wild whoop of joy Grace seized me around the

waist, lifting me and spinning us both, splashing the shallow water into a froth.

"You should not be swinging me around like that," I scolded her through my laughter as she set me down again. "Do you ever listen to the doctor? Are you alright?"

"Oh sweetpea, I am more than alright." Her grin turned wicked. "And I plan to do so much more than just that with you."

The look in her eyes sent a bolt of lightning straight between my legs. Between Grace's injuries and her melancholy, romance had fallen by the wayside. I had to rely on my own fingers for release when I could steal a rare moment of privacy, but I always imagined it was her touch bringing me pleasure.

She took a step closer, our chests almost touching and reached out to cup my cheek.

"If…" Doubt played across her features for a moment. Her sudden insecurity was so raw that it made my heart ache. "If you'll still have me, of course" she murmured.

My lips slammed into hers with more force than I meant but she met my kiss with equal ferocity.

We tumbled backward onto the wet sand, waves still lapping at our entwined bodies and gasped for breath as we broke apart.

"Of course, I shall still have you, you fool," I said, peppering her face with salty kisses.

"That's 'captain fool' to you," she growled with playful menace as her fingers squeezed my jaw and forced my head back, exposing my throat to her attentions. She nibbled and sucked the tender skin with fervor until I was breathless.

Far too quickly, she stopped.

"What are you doing? Why did you stop?" I whined in protest as she grasped my hands and pulled me to my feet.

She grinned as she swept me off the ground and lifted me up in her arms, brushing off my protests that she was going to hurt herself.

"I sometimes forget you are a lady, love. I should treat you better than a crude rut in the sand when I could be taking you to bed instead."

"I am no lady anymore," I reminded her, waggling my eyebrows suggestively as I wound my arms around her neck.

The predatory glint that I so loved lit up her eyes in an instant.

"Are you saying I should fuck you against one of these trees like the filthy little pirate you are then?"

My mouth fell open and my cheeks burned. Even if I were the most adept liar in the world I would not have been able to deny the rush her words instilled in me.

"I'll take that as a yes."

"Please," I gasped.

She set me down instantly. I stumbled slightly but she was already moving, crowding against me and forcing me to back up. I had to grab onto her to stop from falling, her strong arms around me keeping me upright but off balance, guiding me exactly where she wanted me. I squeaked as she shoved me against the hard bark of the palm tree, but the sounds were instantly swallowed by a searing kiss.

"I need you—" I began but her hand wound its way into my hair and jerked my head back so that she could resume what she had started down on the sand.

She gripped me tightly and I groaned as her hot mouth teased my skin. My lower half was drenched in sea water but even without it, I would have been soaked. It had been so long since she had touched me like this that it was driving me to madness.

She must have been thinking the same as she worked her way up until her lips met my ear.

"I missed you."

It was more a breath than a whisper. A sigh. As if desire for me was what filled her lungs instead of air. Again and again on each exhale. *I missed you.*

I could not wait a moment longer. I needed her right then and there. Seizing her hand, I guided it between my legs. Face to face, I saw the moment she felt how much I needed her. Her eyes, as dark and fathomless as they had always been, were fixed to mine and widened as she slid into me with ease and the gasp I had tried to hold back at her touch spilled from my lips.

My hand was between her thighs a moment later. I had dreamt of the feel of her clenching around my fingers many times in the quiet stillness of our little shack but even the sweetest dreams, ones that had me waking dripping and desperate, could not compare.

"I missed you too," I gasped as I rocked against her, grinding myself on the heel of her palm.

"God," Grace moaned as she matched my movements.

The rough bark scraped at me, but the slight sting only made me more ravenous.

We moved in rhythm as if no time had passed, as if we had not endured horrors, as if we knew nothing but each other's bodies. I kissed her with abandon, savoring the taste of her tongue on mine, until the heat in my core rose into my belly and my thighs began to shake. I broke away, panting and moaning as Grace rode my hand harder in response.

"Together," I managed through my labored breathing. I was so close. "Together, Grace."

Her name from my lips was all it took for her to crest the wave of her pleasure and as she spasmed around my fingers with a cry, my own climax took me. I had heard the phrase 'seeing stars', but I had never truly understood until that moment. I shook and writhed against my captain as it took over. I threw my head back and choked out a gasp as I squeezed my eyes closed and color exploded behind my eyelids. In that moment I could have sworn I was flying.

Grace held me close and pressed her forehead to mine as she coaxed the last dregs of my orgasm from me. Dazed, I whimpered as she withdrew her fingers.

"Damn, I had forgotten how fucking beautiful you are when you come," she said, lifting them to her mouth. Languidly, she took them into her mouth and sucked. "And just how good you taste."

"If you get on your knees, you can taste me properly." I put both hands on her shoulders and pushed downwards.

Grace scoffed, but willingly knelt before me. "I had not forgotten how bossy you can be."

"You like it," I sighed as I leaned back against the tree and closed my eyes. Her warm breath caressed my inner thighs as she bunched my skirt up around my waist.

"I do not."

My eyes snapped open. My captain, kneeling at my feet, grinned up at my confused expression wickedly and gave me one slow torturous lick. "I fucking love it."

Just as she was about to get back to the task I had set her, the sound of footsteps made us both freeze and then spring apart.

"Cap'n? Ah there you are!" Petra's gruff voice boomed from the direction of our shack. "What are you— oh for goodness sake!"

As she stomped out onto the beach, she took one look at our flushed faces and dishevelment and rolled her eyes. Grace wiped her mouth on her sleeve, barely hiding her grin.

"Ah it's our honorable first mate. Elise was just telling me the news from the harbor master." Grace winked at me.

"I suppose it's good to see you back to your old self cap'n," Petra said with a scowl. "But save your shenanigans for another time."

"The ship?" The captain's grin dropped instantly, and her eyes narrowed. "What's wrong with my ship, Petra?"

"Calm yourself, Gracie. The ship is fine." Petra spat on the sand and cursed. "It's that woman. Lady something or other that took the both of you before."

"Madame?" I blurted at the same time that Grace snarled, "Rosemary?"

My stomach roiled like it had taken a dive from a towering cliff. I reached for Grace's hand and clung tight as if it were a lifeline. Madame Chevalier still plagued my nightmares, but I had hoped to leave all waking thoughts of my former lover in the same pool of blood I'd left her body in.

"What about her?" Grace's tone was clipped and sharp just like it always was when the subject of that day came up as if the memories pained her to even think about.

"No," I whispered, even though I knew in my bones what was coming. "It cannot be."

"Afraid so, lass." Petra grimaced. "The bitch is alive."

Thank you so much for reading The Bone Heart!
If you enjoyed this book, please consider leaving a
review and following me on social media for future
updates!

Lots of love,

Ivy

Printed in Dunstable, United Kingdom